Arabesque is excited to publish the **Winning Hearts** summer series for 2006, featuring four heroines involved in the world of sports—both as athletes and in relationships with professional sports figures. It is a first for Arabesque, and we hope you enjoy these stories about strong, confident women who find romance and happiness by believing in themselves and trusting their hearts.

In Donna Hill's ***Long Distance Lover,*** world-class runner Kelly Maxwell finds herself at the center of a doping scandal *and* a love triangle. How she resolves her romantic dilemma could ultimately determine the outcome of her career.

When sexy pro quarterback Quentin Williams makes a pass at L.A. assistant D.A. Sydney Holloway, only to be rebuffed—it's more than just his ego that gets bruised. In ***The Game of Love*** by Doreen Rainey, fame and fortune can sometimes mean paying a high price for love.

The world of Major League baseball is tough. But so is Roshawn Bradsher, a feisty divorced single mom with a teenage daughter, in Deborah Fletcher Mello's ***Love in the Lineup.*** So when young hotshot Latin baseball player Angel Rios—who was recruited by Roshawn's ex—suddenly takes an interest in her, it's only the first inning in this home-run romance.

The summer series ends with Gwynne Forster's ***McNeil's Match.*** After a bitter divorce, Lynne Thurston is faced with the prospect of not knowing what to do with the rest of her life, having given up a successful tennis career when she got married. But when she meets Sloan McNeil, all of that changes as he tries to convince her that she still has what it takes to compete—on and off the court.

With bestselling and award-winning authors **Donna Hill, Doreen Rainey, Deborah Fletcher Mello** and **Gwynne Forster** contributing to this series, we know you'll enjoy the passion and romance of these vibrant and compelling characters.

We welcome your comments and feedback, and invite you to send us an e-mail at www.kimanipress.com.

Enjoy,

Evette Porter
Editor, Arabesque/Kimani Press

DONNA HILL

Long Distance Lover

ISBN 1-58314-758-6

LONG DISTANCE LOVER

Long Distance Lover is a work of fiction, and is not intended to provide an exact representation of life, or any known persons in track and field. The author has taken creative license in development of the characters and plot of the story, although track and field events, meets and sites referenced may be real. Arabesque/Kimani Press develops contemporary works of romance fiction for entertainment purposes only.

www.kimanipress.com

Printed in U.S.A.

Prologue

Associated Press—Atlanta
Scandal Rocks Sports World...

Kelly slowly read the headline.

Gold Medal Hopeful Stephanie Daniels Found Dead in her Atlanta Apartment. Kelly's hands shook as she read on. *Following an injury several weeks ago, Kelly Maxwell lost her starting position to Daniels along with her chance at a gold medal. Now it appears that with Maxwell on the mend and her competitor no longer a threat, Maxwell may well regain her golden girl title. However, speculation abounds and the Atlanta police continue their investigation...*

The rest of the words danced and scurried across the page like frightened ants. She tossed the *Atlanta Journal-Constitution* onto the couch in frustration. Her nerves were ragged and the circles under her eyes testified to her lack of sleep.

Ever since the story broke earlier that week the entire track team had been on pins and needles. Investigators from the sports commission had been all over them, digging, probing, wanting to hang something on them—her in particular. She was the star now, the comeback kid, the one in the spotlight, the one they would love to see fall. She was next in line for the starting position on the team—now that Stephanie was gone.

David swore to her that there was nothing to the story—an ugly rumor that had gone haywire, he'd said.

Now, she didn't know what to believe. Too many things didn't add up and what did she didn't like. If everything the papers said was true, her future was over and she had no one to blame but herself.

Moving slowly through her one-bedroom garden apartment in the exclusive Atlanta community, she glanced around at the trophies, the symbols of her accomplishments, the expensive furniture and original artwork, which were all a testament to her ability on the track. Outside her living room window sat a brand-new Navigator, a treat to herself for making it back. In a matter of days, if the stories were true, it could all be gone and she would be hung out to dry.

She picked up her purse from the end table by the door along with her car keys. Her test was scheduled for nine a.m. She opened the front door to flashbulbs and a cacophony of reporters that assaulted her.

"Ms. Maxwell, Ms. Maxwell, what will you do if the tests come back positive?" *Pop, pop, flash, flash.* "Did your coach, David Livingston, have anything to do with this?" "Give us a statement, Ms. Maxwell."

Kelly held her purse up to her face and pushed past the hungry vultures, practically sprinting to her car. She was sure that would be the picture that would wind up on the front page of tomorrow's paper. She jumped into the SUV, put it in gear and sped off, spewing dust and gravel in her wake.

She should have listened to Alex. She should have listened to her heart and stayed in New York.

Chapter 1

Four months earlier

Kelly Maxwell unpacked her gym bag and shoved the contents into her locker. She was pumped. Adrenaline burned in her veins. It had been nearly a month since she'd been able to practice and she was eager to get on the track and cut through the air. Running was her drug of choice. It got her through the days and even some nights when she would sprint through the dark streets of Atlanta when the city was asleep and her only company was the moon and the stars and the wind.

The sounds of approaching laughter and the easy banter shared between friends interrupted her reverie. She shut her locker, turned the key and shoved it into the pocket of her shorts. She'd hoped to have some time alone. She wanted to get in and out before anyone saw her.

"Well, if it's not our little *star* sprinter," Stephanie Daniels said sarcastically, the comment a sneer rather than a compliment. Stephanie walked further into the locker room and looked Kelly up and down. "Pretty soon we're going to have to put STAR on your locker door if David has anything to say about it."

"Stephanie, knock it off," said Maureen, another member of the track team. She flashed Kelly a look of sympathy without letting Stephanie notice.

Stephanie opened her locker and pulled out her bag. "I call them like I see them. She gets the locker room to herself and the track. What next, the coach?" She laughed.

Kelly snatched her towel from the bench and draped it around her neck. "We're all on the same team Stephanie," she said walking up to her. "I'm where I am because it's where I deserve to be." The corner of her mouth curved in a half smile. "And...so...are...you. *Second.*"

She walked out before Stephanie could respond, but she clearly heard herself referred to as a dog of the female persuasion.

When she stepped outside onto the lush field and imagined the empty stadium seats filled to capacity and the crowd roaring her name, Stephanie's ugly innuendos no longer mattered. The only thing that mattered was getting on the track and flying, making all her troubles, her fears, her aloneness vanish under the beat of her feet. Reaching the finish line first is what defined her, made her whole.

She jogged down the steps in David's direction, wincing slightly. She'd have to adjust the wrapping when she got down on the field.

"How's my star today?" David said, putting his arm around her shoulder.

"I wish you wouldn't say that around the other teammates," she said.

He dropped his arm. "Why, because it might make them really step up their game?"

She turned to face him. "No, it makes it difficult for me David…to fit in when everyone thinks I get special treatment."

He looked down into her eyes, and lifted her chin with the tip of his index finger. "Maybe because you are special, Kelly. Ever think of that? I know a winner when I see one. And so does the sports world. I told you that from the first day we met. You are a champion with the medals to prove it. And there's nothing that any of them in the peanut gallery back there can do about that."

She drew in a breath. There was no point in pursuing the subject, David would never understand. They'd been down this road before.

"Now, let's see what you got today." He pulled the towel from around her neck and watched her walk out onto the track. Moments later he followed.

"Need some help with that?" David knelt down beside her.

"I know what I'm doing," Kelly said a bit more harshly than necessary, as she tightened the Ace bandage around her right ankle. She briefly shut her eyes to withstand the pain that shot up her leg all the way to her hip. Slowly she stood up, bouncing on the balls of her feet to test the ankle.

David stood back, his expression tense and hard, marring his usually approachable facade. Kelly Maxwell was his star sprinter, his claim to fame. As much as his heart told him to snatch her off the track and take her home, his drive for the gold medal and all that came with it overrode any pangs of emotion.

He held up his stopwatch. "Ready!"

Kelly assumed her starting position, snatched a glance at him over her left shoulder and gave a short nod.

"Set. Go."

She was off the starting block like a bolt of unexpected lightning, fast, smooth, dazzling to the eye. Kelly was incredible to watch. She moved like a gazelle, the long, lean lines of her body flowing in a rhythm that only came from being a natural athlete. What she did could not be taught. It was instinctive. Every breath she took propelled her faster as if she were inhaling fuel. The power in her legs and arms pulsed with energy as she rounded the turn and came into the home stretch.

David checked the watch. His heart rate escalated. She was on her way to a new record for the 100-meter sprint.

But instead of a cry of victory, a scream that vibrated through his bones echoed in the still morning air. Kelly went down hard on the track, writhing in agony.

David and the team doctor rushed to her side.

"Get a stretcher," David barked to an assistant as he knelt beside her. "It's gonna be okay, Kelly."

"My ankle," she sobbed. "My ankle." She writhed back and forth in pain.

"Take it easy."

Two assistants appeared and gently lifted Kelly off the ground and onto the stretcher.

"Take her straight to Atlanta University Hospital," Dr. Graham said. "I'll meet you there." He turned to David, his blue eyes cold and accusing. "I told you not to let her run." He turned and hurried after his patient.

For several moments, David stood on the empty track as

he listened to the wail of the siren speed off. She was going to be all right, he told himself over and again. She had to be.

David paced the confines of the waiting room, every few minutes checking the wall clock overhead. Time moved at a mind-numbing pace. David knew that the rest of the team was probably speculating on the outcome—Stephanie Daniels in particular. If Kelly was out of the running, Stephanie was the next golden girl in line. It was no secret that Stephanie had no real love for Kelly although she feigned it quite well for the media and anyone of importance who would listen. The truth was, Stephanie believed that Kelly was an overrated has-been whose time had passed and she was merely given special treatment because of David. What Stephanie failed to realize was that Kelly was everything Stephanie only wished she could be.

David stopped short his pacing when Dr. Graham entered the room. His expression was somber.

"David, can I speak with you?"

"How is she?"

"I hope you're satisfied."

"I don't need your sarcasm, Doc. How is Kelly?"

He wiped the sweat from his forehead with the back of his hand, then took off his surgical cap. "She won't be doing any running for quite some time, if ever."

David's breath stopped short in his chest. His features pinched as he stared at the doctor. "What are you saying?"

"Kelly has a hyperextended Achilles tendon and a stress fracture of the ankle."

David shut his eyes and drew in a long, deep breath.

"I told you she wasn't ready to get back on the track."

"It was only a sprain. You said so yourself."

"A serious sprain. The second one in less than six months. The ankle was weak and you knew that. But you let her go out there anyway."

"It was her decision."

"You're her coach!" he said bitterly from between clenched teeth.

David briefly lowered his head then looked into the doctor's eyes. "Does she know?"

"She's hasn't awakened from the anesthesia yet."

"I want to be the one who tells her."

"Why, so you can sugarcoat it and make her believe she's going to be back out on the track in two weeks? I'm sure the surgeon will tell you the same thing since you don't believe anything I say."

David clenched his jaw. He and Dr. Graham had been at odds about Kelly's rehabilitation for months. He didn't expect it to get any better with this latest setback. He'd simply find another doctor for Kelly, one who would give her the encouragement she needed to return to the champion athlete the world had known.

"I want this whole thing kept quiet," David said. "The last thing she needs is the tabloids blowing this out of proportion. Kelly just needs to concentrate on getting well."

Dr. Graham slowly shook his head in disgust. "Always looking at the bottom line, aren't you, David?" He turned and walked away.

David stared at the doctor's retreating back. He needed a plan, a plan to keep this under wraps, to get Kelly out of town as soon as possible, into rehab and with a doctor that saw things his way. In the meantime, he wanted to be the first face that Kelly saw when she woke up.

Chapter 2

Kelly slowly opened her eyes and tried to adjust her vision to the pale walls. She turned her head and tried to move. It was then that she realized her right leg was in a cast up to her hip and suspended from a series of pulleys that looked like something from a torture chamber.

The scent of antiseptic filled her nostrils. She swallowed and started to cough from the dryness in her throat.

The coughing stirred David out of his fitful sleep. He jumped up from the hard plastic chair and went to her bedside. He took her hand.

"K. It's me, David."

"I know who you are David. I didn't hit my head."

He grinned. "Still have your sense of humor, I see."

"I hate to bother you, but could I have some water?"

"Sure. Sure." He rounded the bed to the nightstand and poured her a glass of water from the blue plastic carafe that matched the plastic cup and the plastic chair. The hospital room decor gave David the creeps.

He held the back of her head as she gulped from the cup.

"Thanks." She sank back against the pillows. "So…how bad is it?"

He braced his forearms against the railing of the bed and leaned in close. "There's plenty of time to talk about that. You need to rest."

"Don't play games with me, David. I'm a big girl."

He worked his jaw for a moment. "It will be a while before you can get back on the track. There are pins and braces and all sorts of metal contraptions holding your ankle together."

She squeezed her eyes shut and muttered a curse under her breath. "So I guess this means I'm out of the trials."

He nodded his head. "Yeah, but we are going to get you back in fighting shape in no time. I've already started making some calls."

"Calls? What kind of calls?"

"To rehab centers in New York."

"What? I don't want to go to New York."

"They have the best rehabilitation centers in the country, Kelly. And you are going to have the best. You definitely can't stay in Atlanta. The press wouldn't let you breathe and you know it. It's the only way to keep the wolves at bay."

She started to protest but knew David was right. When she'd been injured six months earlier the press had been so persistent that they actually camped out on her doorstep all night long hoping to get a glimpse of her. They even posed as hospital workers just to get some shots of her. She felt a little shiver at the memory.

David patted her shoulder. "It's going to be alright. I'm with you all the way."

She looked up at him and his smile was full of reassurance. David had been in her corner for as long as she could remember. He was her friend, her mentor, her coach and pretty much the only person she could call family. She relied on him for everything. He believed in her when she didn't believe in herself and the critics tried to downplay her abilities, or cook up one scandal after another about her. He was the one who faced the press when she was too emotionally drained to do so herself. He knew how to get the very best out of her, make her drag things out of herself that she didn't think she was capable of. He'd made her a champion. She owed him. And he knew it.

"I trust you, David. If you think it's best."

He stroked her cheek. "Yeah, I do."

"Does the press know?"

"I'll take care of the press. Don't worry about it. I'll handle it."

"But what about the team? I…"

"Listen, they all know you're the best and they want the best for you. Everyone has been hanging around waiting for you to wake up so that they can tell you how much you mean to the team." He cocked his head over his shoulder. "They're out in the waiting room."

She wiped her eyes. "I must look a mess."

"Not at all," he said softly.

"Tell me anything." She tried to brush back her hair, which she usually wore in a ponytail. Her hair was her one attribute that made everyone take a second look. It was just beyond her shoulders, rich, black and smooth as satin. She owed it all to her great-grandmother who was a full-blooded Cherokee Indian. The American Indian genes seemed to miss everyone else in her family but settled solidly in every fiber of Kelly's being, from the high cheeks and dark piercing eyes to an incredible love for the outdoors and nature. But it hadn't always been that way. She inhaled deeply and pushed the images away.

"Should I let them in?"

Kelly nodded slowly. "Is Stephanie out there?"

"Yes."

Kelly rolled her eyes. "She must be feeling pretty good. This couldn't have worked out better for her if she'd planned it herself."

"K, now is not the time to worry about Stephanie. She'll always be number two. You know it, the team knows it and so do sports fans."

She looked away.

"I'm gonna let them come in for a few minutes and then you get some rest."

Slowly she nodded her head.

Kelly stared up at the off-white ceiling, contemplating her future. The sound of well wishes from her teammates still rang in her ears. She glanced down at her leg and her stomach muscles tensed. Would she ever be able to run again? Was her career, her life over?

She should have listened to her grandmother years ago when she told her that she needed more than "good hair" and speed to get through life. The only profession she'd ever had was that of an athlete. She'd never worked a real job and had no marketable skills. Sure she had a degree in Liberal Arts and that was about as valuable as a three dollar bill. The only way she'd made it through high school and then college was because she could run. What would she do if she couldn't run ever again? The question plagued her throughout the night as her dreams were filled with dismal visions of her watching from the sidelines as life sped past her and when her name was mentioned in sports circles, no one could remember who she was, and she reverted back to the girl who no one hated more than she did.

Chapter 3

"How are you feeling this morning, Kelly?" Dr. Graham asked as he checked the angle of her leg in traction.

"I've felt better, I suppose." She tried to adjust her body in the bed to get more comfortable.

"Let me help you." He came to the top of the bed and adjusted the pillows behind her then pressed the remote to raise the bed.

"Thanks." She looked up at him. "How bad is it really?"

Dr. Graham exhaled a long breath before pulling up a chair next to the bed. "I'm going to be honest with you, Kelly. Brutally so."

She tugged on her bottom lip with her teeth.

"You have sustained what could be a permanent debilitating injury—for an athlete. The damage that has been done to that ankle will take months to recover from and that's not taking rehab into account. And even with the best trainers, I don't believe you will ever be able to run the way you once did."

Her chest constricted. "You're...saying my career is over?"

"Miracles happen every day Kelly. You're a tough young woman and other than a bad ankle you are in good physical condition. Much recovery from any injury, other than the physical, is the mental and emotional. How far you come from this will rely very heavily on you and genetics."

She swallowed over the lump in her throat and slowly nodded her head. "Thank you," she murmured.

"I understand you'll be going to New York for your rehab."

"Yes, David is working that all out."

His cheeks flushed crimson.

Kelly craned her neck forward. "What are you not telling me?"

Dr. Graham looked away then directly into Kelly's eyes, his thick white brows almost forming a single line. "I spoke to David months ago, the last time you were hurt."

Intently looking at him she nodded her head.

"I told him then that you should not get back on the track, that he was sending you out too quickly. Your ankle was still weak. What happened yesterday was unfortunate but inevitable. My concern is the fragility of your bones. It is rare in someone so young." He drew in a breath and stepped closer to her bed. He took her hand. "Kelly, your ankle is like a fragile branch that was set out of doors against the forces of nature much too soon. It didn't get the time or the nurturing that it needed to be at full strength." He clenched his jaw. "David knew this. But he let you go out there anyway."

"It was just as much my fault. I wanted to be on the track. I needed to be out there."

Dr. Graham sighed with resignation. He patted her hand. "Get some rest." He turned to leave.

"How long do I have to stay here?" she asked sounding like a lost child.

"At least a week. They want to be sure that your ankle is setting properly before sending you home."

"When can I start rehab?"

"At least a month. I wouldn't recommend it any earlier than that." He headed for the door, stopped and turned around. "Kelly I would like to run some tests on you."

"Tests? What kind of tests?"

"Some bone density tests and some blood work. I think—"

"That won't be necessary. I'll get all that taken care of when I get to New York. I don't want to have to stay here a minute longer than necessary."

"Be sure that you do, for your own good. No matter what David says." He looked at her for a long moment.

"I will."

A month. She lay in the bed watching the activity of the hospital staff from her doorway. What would she do with herself for a whole month—incapacitated? Tests…there was no telling what the tests would show. Her secret was bound to get out.

She picked up the cup of water from the bedside table and hurled it across the room, barely missing David as he came through the door.

"Was that directed at me?" he asked stepping inside. He reached down and picked up the cup then came toward the bed.

Kelly folded her arms across her chest and looked away,

not wanting David to see the tears of frustration that were burning her eyes.

Gently he touched her shoulder. "What is it, babe? Are you in pain?"

"I'm finished David. Finished." Her voice cracked. "Dr. Graham was just here. He told me everything. I may never run again, not even with rehab." She banged her fist against the mattress. Tears seeped from her closed eyes and rolled down her cheeks. "Christ what am I going to do?"

He leaned down and gathered her in his arms. His heart knocked in his chest. The soft scent of her rushed to his head, the feel of her body in his arms went straight to his groin. Kelly had no idea of the power she had over him. But in all the years they'd worked together, she'd never once indicated an interest in him beyond his coaching ability. He'd watched her move in and out of relationships, each time nothing sticking, and was secretly pleased. His greatest hope was that one day they would consummate their long-standing relationship. He ached to discover what it would feel like to be inside that kind of physical power. For now he would satisfy himself with fleeting moments like this.

"Listen," he said, speaking softly against her hair. "Dr. Graham sees a dark cloud in every rainbow. "We're going to get you the best treatment available and you'll be back on the track and you *will* be a champion. Have I ever let you down?"

She shook her head and sniffed hard.

"Exactly." He smiled. He opened the nightstand and took a tissue from the hospital issued box. "Here."

She wiped her eyes and blew her nose. "Thanks," she murmured. She looked at him. "I need you to be honest with me, David."

"Of course."

"If I can't run again, what will I do?"

Her voice was so pained and the imploring expression in her eyes twisted David's stomach.

"That's not something you're going to have to worry about for a very long time. I promise you."

Chapter 4

David sat at his desk in the office he shared with the assistant coach, poring over the brochure he'd received that morning in the mail from New York. The rehabilitation center at New York University Hospital was one of the best in the country. It was expensive, but worth it. If Kelly were to have any chance of a full recovery he would do whatever was necessary.

A knock on his door took his attention from the information in front of him. He looked up. "Come in." He slid the brochure into his desk drawer.

"Hey, Coach," Stephanie Daniels said, stepping inside. "Mind if I close the door?"

He looked at her with skepticism. The last thing he needed was a harassment suit.

"You can leave it cracked."

She didn't look pleased but did as he asked. She crossed

the room a bit too seductively for David's taste and sat down in a chair on the opposite side of his desk. She crossed her long, bare legs, the micro shorts not leaving much to the imagination. They hugged the apex of her sex defining clearly what she held between her toned thighs. David looked away.

"What can I do for you?"

Stephanie leaned forward revealing a hint of cleavage from her V cut tank top.

"I was just wondering how Kelly is doing."

"She's doing great. She should be released at the end of the week."

"Really?" She toyed with the heart-shaped locket around her neck. "Seems a little soon. She must not be too bad..." She let her statement hang in the air.

David leaned back in his chair. "Kelly will be just fine and back before you know it."

Stephanie twisted her lips and forced a smile. "That's good to hear. Everyone will be glad to have her back."

Everyone but you. "I'm sure."

She stood slowly. "Well, I guess I'd better be going. I have practice in an hour."

"Good."

She hesitated. "Uh, David, not that I'm saying Kelly won't be back...but what if she doesn't?"

He knew what she was hedging at. She wanted Kelly's spot on the team and by all rights it should be hers. But if he admitted that now, he'd have to accept the fact that Kelly may not return. And that he was unwilling to do.

"She will. End of story."

She puffed out her chest. "See you on the track."

"Yeah."

He watched her saunter out. Stephanie Daniels had skill; there was no question about that. But she didn't have star power. Kelly was the whole package, skill and charisma. David had worked with Kelly for the past six years, seeing a champion in her. He'd created her from nothing—turning a shy, insecure girl into a woman who understood the meaning of winning at all costs, who could charm the media and inspire a team. She was his. His career was riding on a championship and Kelly was the key. But if he was forced to deal a new deck of cards to ensure a championship, then he would. He hoped it wouldn't come to that.

Chapter 5

"Let me get the door," David said. He stepped around Kelly and opened the door to her garden apartment.

She inched her way in, awkwardly balancing on crutches, and looked around in awe. The small, very Afrocentrically designed space was filled with flowers. Her living room resembled a tropical hot house, bursting in a kaleidoscope of color.

She turned clumsily toward David, her face beaming in delight. "This is incredible."

"From all the folks who love you."

She moved gingerly into the room and pressed her face to the blossoms, testing one after another. "This is so nice."

"And I'll personally drop by every day to take care of them and you," he added.

"You've done too much already. You haven't missed a

day at the hospital; you brought me home, getting me into rehab. I can't ask you to come over here every day."

"You're not asking. I'm volunteering. I want to and I will." He picked up her small overnight bag. "I'll put this in your bedroom. Why don't you sit down?"

She did as he asked and plopped down on the couch with her leg stretched out in front of her. She propped the crutches against the couch. The delight that she felt only moments ago on coming home slowly slipped away when she considered what she was up against in her current condition. At least in the hospital pretty much everything was done for her. Now she would have to get in and out of bed alone, maneuver through the house—and what about bathing? She sighed and rested her head against the cushions, just as the phone rang.

She reached for the phone on the end table.

"Hello?"

"Kelly Maxwell?"

The voice was totally unfamiliar.

"Who's calling?"

"I'm a reporter from the *Atlanta Journal-Constitution* and I was hoping to speak to Ms. Maxwell."

"She moved." Kelly slammed down the phone just as David returned.

"Who was that?"

"Can you believe it? I haven't been home five minutes and reporters are calling already!" She frowned. "How in the hell do they keep getting my number? I've changed it three times. Do you think they followed us from the hospital?"

David walked over to the window and peeked out. "I don't see anyone, but that doesn't mean they aren't out there. Which is more of a reason for you to get to New York and away from prying eyes." He closed the blinds and joined her on the couch.

Kelly folded her hands on her lap. "You know what, David…"

"What?" He took a seat beside her and angled his body to the side.

"I've never done anything else but run." She laughed lightly. "It seems as long as I can remember I was out in the air trying to slice through it. It paid my way through private high school, got me into college and the endorsements padded my bank account." She turned and glanced at him for a moment. "I'm scared."

"Why?" He reached out and stroked her hair.

"I've never even had a real meaningful relationship, never held a real job. If I'm not running it's almost as if I'm not living. I have dreams of it all disappearing and me along with it. I never thought there would be a time when I'd even have to think about not flying through the wind, hearing the roar of the crowd. I know there is more to life than this. I'm just not sure what it is."

"Kelly, you're young, healthy and you have a long career in front of you."

"Maybe. But I need to be realistic. I need to start thinking about alternatives."

"What are you talking about?"

"If this therapy doesn't work, I need to be prepared for that and I'll need to prepare myself for the real world."

"Hey, hey. What kind of talk is this? You've never been a pessimist. Everything is going to be fine. You'll be back out there before you know it and coming into my office complaining that I work you too hard. Just like old times."

He chuckled and was relieved to see the slight smile brighten her face. "Now that's better."

"You always know what to say."

"Just the truth." He slapped his knee. "How 'bout I whip us up something to eat."

Kelly grimaced. "Uh, the last time you fixed us something to eat we needed the Pepto-Bismol. How 'bout if we order something instead?"

"But I've been practicing," he moaned feigning hurt.

"Well, you just keep at it."

"You wound me." He placed his hand over his heart.

Kelly giggled. "Right. The menus are in the drawer next to the kitchen sink."

"Fine. What do you have a taste for?" He headed for the kitchen.

"Pasta."

"You got it."

While David was gone Kelly wondered how long David would hang around if she couldn't run again.

Chapter 6

When Kelly next opened her eyes, the room was submerged in darkness. She was soaking wet. Her heart raced. She felt exhausted. *Were they still after her?* Panic contracted the muscles in her stomach. She blinked, attempting to clear her head and her eyes. *Had she gotten away?*

She tried to sit up and felt the weight of the cast hold her in place. A thin streak of light filtered in through the partially opened blinds. *Where was she?* She looked wildly around and by degrees her pounding heart slowed. It was only a dream, she realized, a dream that had its genesis in reality, but a dream nonetheless. This was her bedroom in Atlanta, not the back woods of Mississippi, or the alleyways of Chicago's Southside. She was safe here. Home.

Kelly reached for the bedside lamp and the room was bathed in a soft light. The antique shade in a bronze-colored velvet with its dangling clear crystals—a present from her grandmother—cast prismatic shapes against the winter white walls.

Propped up against the lamp was a note. She picked it up and opened it, recognizing immediately David's simple print. She stared at the paper and said each word aloud and slowly.

"'Food in oven. Will call later.'"

She smiled. The always-thoughtful David. She slowly eased her legs over the side of the bed. She reached for her crutches and pushed until she was standing. She made her way into the kitchen and found a Pyrex dish in the oven filled with tender veal cutlet Parmesan and angel-hair pasta. Her stomach grumbled.

After several attempts she was finally able to get the dish out of the oven, while balancing on her crutches and not falling on her face.

She savored every morsel, taking sublime pleasure in each mouthful. It was the first real meal she'd had in a week. But she knew what she'd have to do. She closed her eyes and sighed with pleasure if only for the moment, dropping her fork against the yellow-and-white-checkered plate.

It was times like this, late in the evening when she wished there was more to her life than the next day on the track. She had no real friends or family. Although she had teammates and they went out from time to time, she never felt like one of them, that she was really accepted. For the most part she kept to herself and was ultimately branded a diva. What a joke. *If they only knew.*

Kelly pushed up from the table and took her dish to the sink. She turned on the water and watched as it mixed with the remnants of sauce to gather in a stream of red and disappear down the drain. It was as if she were suddenly watching her life dissolve in front of her. All that she'd endured, all that she'd worked for could wash away like the sauce on her plate, disappearing into a black hole of no return—unless she fought back. All she had was her skills. She wouldn't lose the only thing in life that she'd ever succeeded at—not without a fight.

The phone rang.

She ambled over to the wall phone. "Hello?"

"I know it's late, but I wanted to check on you."

"David." Her insides warmed.

"Did you get your dinner?"

"Yes, I did. Thank you. How…did I get in my room?"

"I carried you. You were totally out of it and I didn't want to wake you. And I certainly didn't want you to fall off the couch."

She laughed. "I didn't hear a thing."

"You need your rest. It's one of the best remedies for any ailment. Do you need anything? I can drive back over if you do."

As much as she wanted the company she declined. "I'm fine. Really."

"Well, I'll be there in the morning."

"Don't you have to be at practice?"

"Reggie can run the team through the drills. I don't want you to be alone."

She didn't want to read more into what he said. He was only offering his help to an injured member of his team. He would do the same for any of them.

"I'll call you when I get up."

"Make sure that you do," he said. "I'll see you tomorrow."

"Okay."

"Good night, K."

"Good night."

Thoughtfully she hung up the phone. She'd known David since she was seventeen years old and he was standing at the finish line when she'd won her race at a high school track meet.

"You're good, but I can make you better," he'd said by way of introduction.

She bent in half to catch her breath and looked up at him. "Who are you?"

"Your future coach." He grinned and her heart did a funny little dance in her chest.

"You seem pretty sure of yourself."

"I am."

She stood up and braced her hands on her hips. "How do you know I want a coach?"

"Because you want to be a winner." He handed her a towel.

She stared at it for a moment before taking it and wiping her face. "Thank you."

"So what do you say? If you want me to talk to your family, I will."

"There's no one to talk to. Thanks for the towel and the offer. But forget it." She handed him back the towel, turned and jogged away before he could react.

But as Kelly soon discovered, David was as determined as he was handsome and that was saying something. David Livingston was tall and lean, his features angular but with the kind of even brown complexion that women slaved to maintain. His smile was as generous as his eyes and his deep laughter reminded her of winter nights sitting in front of a fireplace.

He showed up for every track meet. He was the loudest in the stands as she jetted to the finish lines. David became a fixture to a point where she looked for him in the stands, listened for his cheers among the crowd.

Finally one day after practice she walked up to him.

"Okay, I give up. What can you do for me?"

"That's what I wanted to hear."

They'd been a "team" ever since.

But not even David knew all her secrets.

Slowly she went into the bathroom, pulled up the toilet seat and stuck her finger as far down her throat as she could.

Chapter 7

"This wheelchair is a bit much, David," Kelly said as he pushed her through the terminal of American Airlines.

"You may be fast as lightning on the track, my dear, but you need a little work with the crutches. I want to get to the hotel sometime today."

"Very funny."

They trailed behind a redcap who pushed a metal cart that was loaded with their baggage.

"There's a car waiting for us out front. We'll have you settled in no time." David weaved in and out of the flow of human traffic mindful of his precious cargo.

As always JFK airport was bustling with activity. The press of people in myriad attire, speaking in every imaginable language, was an awesome experience. The airport was a microcosm of humanity. Voices from unseen sources called out a steam of flights to everywhere in the known world, periodically interspersed with warnings about unattended baggage and the consequences of taking packages from persons unknown to you. A montage of aromas stampeded through the food court reminiscent of raucous stadium revelers doing a victory dance. The occasional National Guard patrolled the walkways, a holdover from 9/11.

"At least they cut the cast down," Kelly said as they made it toward the exit doors. "I never would have made it through this crowd to the flight with my leg sticking out a mile in front of me."

"It's progress. I told you that you would be back in no time. It's only been four weeks and look how far you've come."

"Although this space boot isn't a fashion statement."

David chuckled and pushed open the glass doors.

The first blush of New York City welcomed them with a cool breeze and a spring shower.

A middle-aged man decked in a black suit, striped shirt and shiny black tie stood in front of a silver stretch limo holding up a sign with David's name on it.

"Right here," David instructed the redcap, pointing to the driver.

"Welcome to New York, Mr. Livingston, Ms. Maxwell. I'm your driver Bill." He turned to Kelly. "Let me help you into the car ma'am."

"I can—"

But before she'd finished her sentence, he'd lifted her from the wheelchair as if she were no heavier than a bag of rice and gently put her in the back seat.

"There's juice, soda, snacks and the buttons above you control the music, DVD player and the air," Bill said before backing out of the car door. He straightened and turned to David who immediately held up his hands.

"I think I can get in by myself."

"Of course, Mr. Livingston." He stood aside.

David got in and sat opposite Kelly. "Efficient," he muttered then shut the door behind him.

Kelly giggled. "I thought for sure he was gonna pick you up, too."

David reached for a bottle of chilled water from the bucket of ice. "So did I. But we would have had to fight." He twisted off the top then took a long swallow. "Aaah. You okay?" He took another gulp.

"Fine." She propped her leg up along the length of the wraparound leather seating.

The motion of the car rocked them gently against the plush interior. Kelly looked out the tinted windows as the landscape of the Big Apple spread out in front of her. Buildings rose toward the cloudy skies, murky silhouettes against the light gray backdrop. She was missing home already.

"How much do you know about this doctor-therapist, whatever he is?" she asked tersely.

"I checked Dr. Hutchinson's credentials thoroughly. He's worked with plenty of athletes. He's one of the best."

Kelly looked away. "How long do we have to stay here?"

"Until you're better." He glanced at her profile. Her mouth was a tight line as it always was when she was upset, worried or concentrating on the track. This was not the track. "You want to tell me what's really bothering you?"

"Nothing," she muttered.

"Everything will be fine. You'll see."

She folded her arms. "Sure."

"Hungry?"

"No."

"You really haven't been eating lately. Are you sure you're okay?"

"I'm fine. Please stop asking me."

"All right, all right. Take it easy."

She pushed out a breath. "I'm sorry. Guess my nerves are getting the best of me."

David leaned over and took her hand. "Look at me."

Reluctantly she did.

"Haven't I always taken care of you?"

"Yes."

"Have I ever let you down?"

"No."

"Then that's all you need to remember."

"But what if someone finds out?"

"They won't. They won't," he repeated. "All you have to do is follow the instructions of the therapist and the rest will take care of itself."

The car slowed then came to a stop. Moments later, Bill opened the door. David got out first, went around to the trunk and retrieved Kelly's crutches. Together he and Bill helped her from the car.

"What…no wheelchair?" Kelly quipped while gaining her balance.

"Time is no longer of the essence."

Bill signaled the bellhop and they loaded the luggage onto a cart.

The decor of the Marriott was gracefully elegant. A dazzling chandelier hanging from the vaulted ceiling was the centerpiece of the circular floor. Light touches of gold filigree graced tables, the edges of counters and the reception desks. The hotel was busy. There was a steady movement of guests and uniformed hotel staff, but not one seemed to pay Kelly any undue attention. In a town like New York, celebrities were a dime a dozen.

"Welcome to the Marriott," the concierge greeted. "I hope you have a lovely stay with us and if there is anything we can do to make you more comfortable, Ms. Maxwell, please let me know."

"Thank you, I will."

"If you will follow me, I'll personally escort you to your room. You're all checked in."

"You have her in the presidential suite, correct?" David asked.

"Of course. Only the best. And it has the connecting suite as you requested."

David nodded. "Excellent."

"Connecting suite?" Kelly mouthed to David.

"We'll talk upstairs."

Once they were settled and the concierge had bowed his way out, Kelly didn't waste a moment in getting to the connecting suite situation.

"You want to tell me now?"

"Look, I plan to be here for the next two weeks. You're going to need help. What sense does it make for me to be in a completely different room, possibly on a different floor, in case of an emergency?"

She'd have to be extra careful. David must never know. There were many things she shared with David, but this could not be one of them. No one must find out. She was too ashamed.

"Fine. I suppose you're right. Just make sure you knock first."

He chuckled. "The door locks from your side."

Her lips flickered ever so slightly until they formed the halo of a smile. She half walked, half hopped toward the couch and sat down. She looked up at him then stretched out her hand.

David walked toward her, took her hand then sat down. "What?" His voice was a gentle nudge.

"If I haven't told you thank you—then thank you—for everything. I don't know how many strings you had to pull to get me here. I did my research, too. This Dr. Hutchinson is booked through the year."

He tightened his hold on her hand and looked her deep in the eyes. "I told you, whatever needed to be done to help you I was going to make it happen."

Kelly lowered her gaze. "I owe you so much." She looked up and stared into his eyes.

David felt himself being pulled into the midnight pools of her eyes. It would be so easy to kiss her right at that moment. Easy to loosen the barrette that held her hair in place and watch it fall in waves across her shoulders. So easy to lean her back against the pillows of the couch and caress the skin that he knew would feel like satin beneath his fingertips.

David forced a smile. "I'd better unpack." Quickly he stood before desire outweighed reason. "Why don't you order room service? Let's see if the hotel lives up to all its hype." He started to walk toward the door that separated them. "I'll be back in a few."

Kelly didn't trust herself to speak so she simply nodded her head. Once David closed the door behind him, she finally released the breath she'd held. How was she going to be able to get through the next two weeks with David less than one hundred feet away every night?

Chapter 8

Dr. Alex Hutchinson strolled casually down the corridor of New York University Hospital, while studying the chart he held in his hand.

Kelly Maxwell. 29. Track star… He reviewed the details of her injury and his gut instinct and years of experience told him only a miracle would have her running again, at least competitively.

"Dr. Hutchinson, good morning," said Ruby Rivers, his assistant, falling in step next to him.

Ruby had been assigned to him since he started at NYU six years earlier. She was bright, hardworking and totally no nonsense. Over the years they'd grown from working companions to best friends. Ruby was the older sister he never had. Alex relied on Ruby's mother wit and sense of humor on more days than he could count. He knew she was probably near fifty but she didn't look a day over thirty.

"Aren't we being formal today," Alex commented, flipping the page on the chart.

"Have to keep up appearances, Hutch. Wouldn't want the staff to think that you were actually nice enough to have friends." She winked. "So who do we have today?"

"Kelly Maxwell."

"*The* Kelly Maxwell—the track star?"

"One and the same."

Ruby took the chart from Alex. Her dark brown eyes quickly scanned the pages.

"Hmm. Serious injury." She looked up at Alex, then handed back the chart.

"You don't usually see this kind of injury in someone her age and what I would assume to be in good health."

"My thought, too."

"We'll take a look and map out a plan like always." He glanced down at her and smiled. "Miracles happen every day."

"If anyone down here on earth can pull off a miracle, it's you."

"Flattery like that will get you a free lunch."

"That's what I was batting for."

"How well I know you, Ms. Ruby."

Kelly came to a halt in front of the hospital doors. "There's going to be forms to fill out." Her full features were pinched tight.

David put his hand on her shoulder and squeezed gently. "I'll take care of it."

"Are you sure?"

"Stop worrying. Just get better." He kissed the top of

her head. "Come on, let's get you inside, we're causing a traffic jam standing here like this."

"We're here to see a Dr. Hutchinson," David said to the nurse at the circular reception desk.

"Name?"

"Kelly Maxwell," David said.

The nurse typed in the information in the computer, then took a set of forms and attached them to a clipboard. "Ms. Maxwell will need to complete these. As soon as she's done I'll send her in. What kind of insurance does she have?"

David gave her the name of the insurance carrier, and then took the clipboard. He joined Kelly on the bench.

"Here, you need to fill these out."

Panic lit her eyes like fireflies in a night sky.

He sat beside her. "Fill in your name on the first line and check 'no' for all of the questions," he instructed in a low voice.

She pressed her lips together in concentration, forming one letter after the other. Today was worse than usual. Stress.

What seemed more like hours than minutes, Kelly put the pen down and handed the papers to David.

He smiled. "You did good," he whispered. "I'll give this to the nurse and be right back."

Kelly watched David walk away then engage in lively conversation with the nurse. She twisted her hands in her lap. Perspiration began to dot her forehead. She wanted to run but she couldn't. The contents of her stomach rose to her throat. She felt ill, always did at times like this—especially over the last two years when the stress and pressure of competition had escalated.

It began with the feeling of panic, as if the walls were

closing in on her, followed by waves of nausea that would only subside after ingesting large amounts of food, only for her to purge it all. It was a vicious, ugly cycle that had become a part of her life. A part that she kept hidden from everyone, even David. Sometimes panic wasn't even the catalyst to set her off. It could be anything, anything that made her remember the young girl she'd once been. *Run, Kelly, run. Jeering laughter*. She ran faster, as fast as she could to get away from her tormentors—the girls and the boys who reveled in her misery.

One day she swore she'd run so far and so fast they'd never be able to catch her. But for now she just needed to get away. *Run, Kelly, run.*

"Are you okay?" David placed a gentle hand on her shoulder.

Her head snapped up. Her eyes darted left then right. This wasn't Mississippi. She wasn't running through the fields, through the swamps. There was no one after her. She'd outrun them all.

Her heartbeat gradually slowed to its normal rhythm.

"Yeah, fine. Just daydreaming, I guess. Um, would you mind getting me a cup of water?"

"Sure."

David walked the few feet toward the vending machine, stepping around a young man with a prosthetic leg who was slowly limping past him. Accident or casualty of war? He didn't know. Either way it was a damned shame. The kid couldn't have been more than twenty. Sadder still were all the others who half walked, wheeled or hopped along in various stages of rehabilitation. The waiting area vibrated with the sounds of metal wheels clanging across the linoleum floors or the squeak of rubber-tipped crutches finding traction.

He dropped four quarters into the machine. A bag of corn chips dropped into the tray. He snorted at the irony. Life was all about the luck of the draw, getting the right combination, and praying that when you dropped your coins in the slot of life you got what you needed, what you'd paid your dues for.

David dug into his pocket, pulled out a dollar and put it in the machine. This time he got the water.

"Here you go."

"Thanks." She twisted off the top and took two long swallows. That was better. Her stomach muscles relaxed. "Did the nurse say how long?"

David checked his watch then stepped aside as an orderly pushed a wheelchair-bound woman down the hall. "Shouldn't be any more than a few minutes."

"Ms. Maxwell…"

"Yes?"

"The doctor will see you now. Treatment room seven. Straight down the hall."

"See." He helped her to her feet. David walked slowly beside her. "Ready?"

She nodded. "Let's do this."

He grinned. "That's my girl."

Chapter 9

Alex stood when Kelly, followed by David, walked through the door.

"Ms. Maxwell." Alex approached. He extended his hand then realized his faux pas. "I'm Dr. Hutchinson." He was oddly transfixed by her and didn't know why. Was it the look of uncertainty in her dark eyes or the cascade of ebony hair that brushed her slender shoulders, framing not a beautiful face by any standards but a rather plain one? Her face was a puzzle of exotic and very ordinary all mixed together.

"I'm David Livingston. Kelly's coach."

Alex focused on David. "Mr. Livingston." He shook David's hand.

"Call me David."

Alex nodded but didn't offer the same familiarity in return. Kelly had yet to speak.

She hopped over to the chair and sat down without a word,

thinking that the fabulous Dr. Hutchinson was really the actor Blair Underwood in a lab coat. Dark, handsome, boyish good looks with a maturity that would never age and a subtle sex appeal that wafted around him like a good cologne.

Alex pressed his lips together and exhaled a short laugh. "Why don't we get started? I've gone over your chart and your X-rays." He perched on the edge of his desk. "Can you tell me what happened?"

"Is that really necessary?" David interjected.

Alex turned his gaze toward David. "Whenever I work with a patient, I like to know as much about them as well as everything that led up to them having to see me." The left corner of his mouth curved in an expression that was a challenge more than a grin.

"I was practicing," Kelly suddenly said.

Both men turned toward her.

She cleared her throat. "I was getting ready for the trials…the Olympic trials."

"Next summer right?"

Kelly nodded her head in agreement.

Alex smiled. "Former track and field groupie." He rested his arms on his thighs. "You want to tell me what happened?" he asked gently.

Kelly told him about that day on the track while David stood in the corner with a petulant scowl on his face and his arms folded.

"I have to be honest with you," he began once Kelly finished. "The injury that you sustained is quite severe for someone with no previous breaks and for someone in good physical condition. You didn't step on anything or remember twisting it in an odd way?"

"No. I was running the way I always do. When I made the final turn..." She winced at the memory.

Alex stood. "Okay. We'll want to run a few tests before we get started and get some new MRIs of that ankle. How does it feel when you put pressure on it?"

"Not bad. More of an ache than a pain."

There was a knock on the door.

"Come in."

"Good morning." Ruby looked from Kelly to David.

"This is my assistant, Ruby Rivers. You'll be working with her during your rehab."

"My understanding was that you would be Kelly's physician, not an assistant," David said. He said the last word like a curse.

Ruby arched a brow and her neck reflexively jerked back like in her days in the East New York projects.

"Ms. Rivers is a licensed and certified physical therapist. She is the one I'd go to should the need ever arise." He stepped over to Kelly. "I'll see you in about an hour after Ruby runs a few tests and takes some information." He walked to the door and pulled it open. "Mr. Livingston, can I speak with you a moment?"

"I want to wait until Ms. Rivers is done. There may be some questions I can answer."

Alex glanced in Kelly's direction and caught the flash of panic that widened her eyes. "She'll be fine with Ruby," he said faltering a bit, caught off guard by the expression on Kelly's face. He put his hand on David's shoulder and ushered him out. "We can talk in the lounge."

"I've been a fan of yours for a while," Ruby said.

Kelly offered a faint smile.

"Must be tough being in the spotlight."

Kelly didn't respond.

"I'm going to take some blood." She cleaned Kelly's arm at the bend of her elbow, prepared the needle and drew two vials of blood.

Kelly looked away until Ruby was finished. Ruby bent Kelly's arm toward her chest while pressing a sterile gauze at the site of the tiny puncture.

"Just hold that in place for a few minutes." She put the vials on a tray and filled out two labels. "I really am quite good at what I do." She turned to Kelly. "And Hutch is even better." She smiled.

"Hutch?"

"Yes, Dr. Hutchinson. Everyone around here calls him Hutch."

"Oh." Kelly smiled, running the name and the image of the man around in her mind.

"He's worked with some of the greats, from basketball stars to jockeys, and got them back out there," she assured, hoping to ease the lines of tension that framed Kelly's dark eyes.

Kelly released a long sigh. "Running is all I've ever known," she said softly.

"One thing my mama always told me was never put all your eggs in one basket. I originally went to school for interior design. Thought I was the next great B. Smith." She chuckled. "I struggled for about five years when I realized it wasn't for me or I wasn't for it."

"So how did you decide on therapy?"

"My mom had a hip injury about ten years ago. And the doctors really botched it. I had to move back home to help her. I had to learn things just to help her get through her day. I got really interested in the recovery process and didn't want to see anyone go through what my mother went through. So I went back to school. I actually studied under Hutch. And the rest, as they say, is history."

"How long do you think I'll have to be here?"

"That all depends on how well you do during the rehab and the extent of your injury. We'll work with the ankle and the whole body. You'll be put on a specific exercise regime along with a diet."

Her heart thumped. "Diet?"

"Absolutely. We want to make sure your body has everything it needs to rebuild and become as strong as it can be. The instructions are easy to follow."

Diet. Instructions. She hadn't figured on that.

Chapter 10

Alex walked alongside David, guiding him down the busy corridor with a lift of his chin or a pointed finger toward their destination. He definitely wanted to keep what he intended to say away from prying ears.

Once inside the doctor's lounge, Alex did a quick visual to ensure they were alone before closing the door.

They were about the same height and weight, Alex calculated. He'd take him standing up.

Alex clasped his hands in front of him. "You seem to have a problem, Mr. Livingston. You want to tell me what it is?"

David clenched his jaw and took a step toward Alex who almost laughed at the veiled challenge.

"My only interest is Kelly's well-being. I want her to get the best care possible. And since I'm footing the bill, I want to be informed of every iota of her treatment."

"I see." Alex lowered his gaze for an instant before

moving toward David. "You brought her here because of the level of treatment I can provide, the reputation of this hospital and the results of our patients. The reason why all of that works, *Dave*, is because we have the complete confidence of the patient. This is impossible to accomplish if we have someone hovering around and second-guessing everything we do." He walked around David, forcing him to turn. "Now if you have a problem with that then as much as it pains me to say this, I suggest you take Ms. Maxwell to another facility."

Alex glared at him, weighed his options. They were limited.

"I expect to be updated weekly."

"That's fair enough. I'm sure Kelly will be able to keep you up to speed." He paused. "You're aware that by law, I'm not required to tell you anything. So if Kelly agrees in writing—then we will keep you in the loop—to a point. However, the final decisions have to be hers. She's my patient, not you and not the Gold Medal club."

David took a gulp of pride. It burned on the way down. Hutchinson was the best in the country. He didn't have to like Hutchinson for him to do a good job. If they left and went back to Atlanta, the press wouldn't leave her alone. And he had too much going on for the press to be all over them like gnats.

"Fine. Whatever it takes for Kelly to be well."

Alex folded his arms. "How long have you been her coach?"

"A little more than ten years." A faint smile played around the deep corners of his mouth. "Spotted her in her freshman year of high school. Was able to wrangle an athletic scholarship, got her out of that dump of a school and into a private high school."

"Commendable. What did you get out of it?"

The pleasant smile disappeared. "What makes you think I was out to get anything?"

"Altruism isn't a popular human trait. Everyone does what they do for a reason—to get something out of it, even if it's no more than to feel good."

"Is that your excuse—for the white coat and the arrogance?"

Alex laughed from deep in his gut and lounged against the door frame. "Yeah. Pretty much. There's nothing like a man in uniform with a little power to wow the ladies."

"A doctor with an inflated sense of humor and ego. Just what we need more of."

"The world would be a better place. But, enough about me, back to you. That's a pretty long time to be in someone's life. You must be close—like family."

"Very."

It was a challenge that Alex felt like taking. "Maybe it's more—"

The knock on the door cut him off in mid-sentence. He stepped back from the door and opened it.

Ruby wrinkled her nose and sniffed. "Is that testosterone I smell in here?" she asked in a stage whisper.

"Not funny."

"Your patient is ready." She tiptoed and spoke to David over Alex's right shoulder. "It will be at least an hour maybe more, Mr. Livingston. If you want to go and come back…" She let her sentence drift off.

"Thanks, but I think I'll wait."

Alex turned to him. "Feel free to hang out in here. It's much more comfortable than the waiting room. Anyone asks, just tell them you got the okay from me." He grinned.

The last thing David wanted to be was in debt for a favor, even one as minor as this. He waved off Alex's offer. "Thanks, but I'll wait up front with everyone else. It's not a problem."

Alex shrugged. "See you in a few, then." He walked out with Ruby at his side.

David stared at their backs before heading out. His eyes tightened. His jaw locked. Hutchinson was going to be a problem. The sooner Kelly got well and out of there the better.

Chapter 11

Kelly jumped when the door opened. Instinctively she pulled the hospital gown tighter around her body, a body that was rubber band tight, stretched to the limit and had just snapped.

"Sorry to keep you waiting, Ms. Maxwell," Alex apologized.

"Where's David?"

She sounded childlike asking for a parent or guardian—or lover. Alex crossed the room to where she was perched atop the exam table. *Just how close were they? Better question: why did it matter?*

"He's in the waiting room, waiting."

Kelly shifted. "I'd prefer if he was here with me." She looked straight at Alex then Ruby.

Alex hesitated for a moment before saying the first thing that came to his mind, which he was prone to do. For example he really wanted to ask her what the hell she was so frightened of and if she'd ever slept with David Livingston. Both questions were inappropriate, so he kept them to himself. And was proud of his effort.

"There's really nothing to worry about. I'm relatively harmless." He gave her his best "I'm really charming" smile.

Ruby chuckled lightly to shoo the tension aside. "Generally family and friends are more of a problem than the patients. I've had folks faint or run out of the room to relieve themselves of breakfast or lunch."

Kelly's raven eyes widened with alarm. "I thought you said it wasn't that bad."

"It isn't. It just looks that way," Alex said, sitting on the stool in front of the examination table.

Ruby handed him Kelly's chart. He put it on his lap and focused on Kelly, whose expression vacillated between fear and defiance. Something didn't sit right with him.

"Ms. Maxwell, one thing I want to assure you of, my only job is to get people well—as well as they can be. But in order to do that I need them to believe in me and in themselves. I told your bodyguard—uh, David—as much." He gently lifted her leg. "When did they put this on?" he asked referring to the space boot.

"About a week ago. And he's not my bodyguard."

Alex glanced into her face but didn't comment.

He ran his hands up and down her leg yet even with the cast and the boot a tingling thrill erupted in the base of her stomach and spiraled down her legs. Her inner thighs trembled. It wasn't lost on Alex.

He gazed up at her. His eyes said "trust me." Her nostrils flared and she jutted her chin forward.

"I believe in myself," she said in a hoarse whisper. "And before this is all over, you'll believe in me, too."

Slowly he stood and lowered her leg, never breaking contact with her eyes. He stepped closer and put his arm around her waist to help her down and his fingers inadvertently slipped between the open folds in the back of the gown.

Her skin ignited beneath the tips of his fingers and she drew in a sharp breath.

"Are you okay?"

"Yes," she stammered.

It was only an instant that he held her, but to Kelly it was a sensual dance, that one moment that girls dream of.

Alex eased her to her feet. He cleared his throat along with his head. "Um, as soon as I get the report back from your MRI and blood work we can start on your rehab program."

Kelly nodded, uncertain of her voice.

"'Scuse me," Ruby interrupted. She shot Alex a "what the devil are you doing" look. "I'm going to schedule Ms. Maxwell to return on Wednesday. The labs and the MRI will be back by then."

Alex's lids flickered as if slowly awakening from a daydream. "Sure." He reached for Kelly's crutches then slowly released his hold on her waist once she was steady on her feet.

"Thanks."

He stepped back. "Okay, so we'll see you on Wednesday. Ruby will get you into X-ray and then over to the waiting room."

Ruby held the door open while Kelly moved toward it.

Kelly glanced over her shoulder at Alex before leaving.

Ruby rolled her eyes at him and shut the door behind them.

* * *

Alex sat on the edge of the exam table flipping through Kelly's chart. But he wasn't seeing the words in front of him. Instead he was remembering the feel of her bare skin beneath his fingers. Accident or Freudian slip; he didn't know. But whatever it was he couldn't let it happen again. He'd made that mistake once before with Leigh and had no intention of a repeat performance.

Leigh Wells had nearly cost him his career. She'd come to him after surviving a horrific car accident. Her right leg was broken in three places and she'd had to learn to walk all over again. He spent every day with her for three months. And during that time he'd given into his greatest weakness—the female body.

Leigh was gorgeous, a model with a body to fall at her feet for. Lust and temptation outweighed his good judgment when he started making house calls well after business hours. Leigh welcomed him with open arms and open other things as well. He used all of his skills, every technique available to him to return Leigh back to the woman she once was. But nothing he did would eliminate the lifelong pain she would endure or the permanent limp. Her career was over and so was their relationship. The day he told her there was nothing else he could do was a day he'd never forget.

They were in bed together having just made love. It was near midnight in the middle of the summer. So hot you could barely breathe. The air conditioning was at its highest but they were soaking wet and sated. Alex peeled himself off the wet sheets to get a cigarette from the dresser on the other side of the room. He found his pack of Newports and lit up. He turned to offer one to Leigh and was stopped cold by the erotic vision in front of him.

Leigh was stretched out on the bed, completely naked—the sheet tossed to the floor. The stream of light from the moon cast a halo of sorts around her body making her look like a dream. Her knees were bent. Her thighs spread wide. Her hands stroked herself.

"I'm not quite finished," she said in a voice that drifted through the dimness and licked his warm flesh.

Alex grinned. Leigh was insatiable and he loved to oblige her craving.

"I would come and get you but walking is difficult to say the least, especially after a session with you."

Alex crushed out his cigarette and joined her on the bed. He caressed her right breast.

"It's been six months, Hutch." She stroked his thigh, moving higher until she held his hardening penis in her hand. She caressed it the way she knew he liked, flicking her finger across the head and relished the sound of his quick intake of breath. "I can't stand this anymore," she murmured in a husky whisper and for an instant Alex wasn't sure if she meant waiting for session two or something else. "I want to be the woman I was," she was saying, pulling him back to reality. "I want to be able to walk like normal."

"Leigh…" This was the moment he'd been dreading. "I…"

She sat up, dropping the contents in her hand as if stung. "What is it?"

"There's nothing else that can be done."

She laughed but it sounded ill. "Nothing to be done! What the fuck are you talking about?"

"We've done everything we could."

"You're telling me that I'm going to go through the rest of my life as a gimp in a brace, popping pain pills?" Her voice escalated in incredulity with every word." Her amber eyes flashed with anger and disbelief.

"I've done all I can, Leigh. You know that."

"You promised me I would be fine, that I would walk again!"

"Leigh..." He reached for her and she smacked his hand away.

"Don't fuckin' touch me! You promised me I would walk again."

Her chest heaved in and out and even in the dimness of the room he could see the sparkle of tears hanging on her cheeks.

"You are a strong beautiful woman. You will get through this."

"What am I supposed to do with the rest of my life, Hutch? Tell me that. Tell me, you bastard!" She picked up a pillow from behind her and threw it at him. "Modeling, that's me. It's what I do. When was the last time you saw a model strut down a runway with a leg brace and crutches?"

She wept openly, screaming out her fury at the injustice of it all and the rage she felt toward Alex.

"You promised me," she said from deep in her throat. She swiped at her face with the back of her hand. "And you lied."

"Leigh..."

"Get out! Get out!"

He snatched up his pants and boxers from the floor where he'd tossed them earlier and gabbed his T-shirt from the back of the chair.

"I'm sorry. I should have told you as soon as I knew,"

he said as he got dressed. "But I still had hope. I thought I could fix everything."

She looked up at him through eyes filled with tears. "I don't want to ever see you again. Ever."

"Are you sure this is what you want, Leigh?"

"It is." She folded her arms beneath her breasts and looked away as Alex walked out.

The next time he saw Leigh was three weeks later. Her face made the front page of the *Daily News*. "Supermodel Found Dead—Suicide."

At times, some of the strangest times, he would see her face on that last night and when he least expected it, the weight of guilt would nearly cripple him and he'd spend days locked in his one bedroom apartment trying to drink away the memories.

After Leigh's death he'd gone to the chief resident Bert Logan, who was more like a father than a boss, and submitted his resignation. It was immediately rejected. Between Bert and Ruby, they'd eventually talked him out of it.

That was five years ago. For the most part, he'd put it behind him, slowed down on blaming himself and worked every day at regaining his confidence—and he had—until today.

He hopped down off the exam table, tucked Kelly Maxwell's chart beneath his arm and walked out.

Until today.

Chapter 12

David slid his plastic card through the slit, opening the door to the suite. He stepped aside to let Kelly pass.

For the entire twenty-minute ride back from the hospital, he'd been in a state of contained fury. But glass partition or not, he wasn't going to spew his raw feelings all over the back of the limo.

The moment Kelly heard the door close behind her she turned on David. "You want to tell me what the hell is bugging you? You looked like you were sitting on a tack for the whole ride." She rested her crutches against the edge of the couch and slowly sat down holding on to the arms of the couch for support.

David pulled off his chocolate colored suede jacket and tossed it onto the empty love seat. He paced in front of her. "I don't like him," he finally spat out.

"Who?" she asked already knowing the answer.

"Hutchinson, that's who. He's an arrogant sonofabitch, and I don't like him."

Kelly pressed her lips together forcing herself to think first before she shot out how stupid David sounded. She gingerly folded her hands in her lap.

"Really. You were the one who 'highly' recommended him. Said he was the best."

"I know what I said," he snapped. He walked over to the wet bar, went behind the counter and fixed himself a quick rum and coke, no ice. He took a long swallow before responding. "I'm having second thoughts. I think we need to find someone else."

"You've got to be kidding. It's a little late in the game, don't you think? We've packed up, left Atlanta, come all the way to big bad New York City and because you 'don't like him' you want to find someone else. Do you know how ridiculous that sounds?"

He clenched his teeth before finishing off his drink then walked toward her. He knelt down and placed his hands on her knees.

"Listen, you know I only want the best for you. I have a bad feeling about him."

"I don't."

"You wouldn't."

"What's that supposed to mean?"

"You're a woman."

Her brows shot up. "Meaning?"

"Meaning I can see through him."

"David, you're not making any sense."

He pushed up and stood. "We're going back to Atlanta."

"No. We're not."

He looked down at her, saw the same determination in

her eyes that she had on the track moments before a big race. "I know what's best for you."

"And I don't? David, I'm not sixteen anymore. I'm a grown woman. I'm capable of making my own decisions—if you'd ever let me," she added and didn't flinch when he took a step toward her. "I'm staying."

David heaved a sigh. His features hardened.

"You said he was the best. We'll never know if we leave. I want to run again and I believe he can make that happen."

He shoved his hands in his pockets. She was right. There was no question about Hutchinson's credentials. He had to put his personal dislikes aside for Kelly's sake.

"Fine," he conceded on a long breath. "If this is what you want." His stern expression softened and the hint of a smile curved his mouth. "You know I can't deny you anything." He reached over and tucked a wayward strand of hair behind her right ear.

"Thank you. I will be fine. I feel it."

"We'll give it a shot." He walked to the love seat and picked up his jacket, draped it over the bend of his arm. "Can I get you anything? I'm going to order room service."

"No. Thanks."

He gave her an incredulous look. "You haven't eaten all day. You should be starved by now."

"Maybe later."

He stared at her for a moment.

"What?"

"Nothing," he muttered. "I'll check on you later."

Kelly waited until she was sure David was settled in his room before she got up and went into her bedroom.

She went to the dresser and fished beneath her underwear

and pulled out a bag of candy, chocolate bars and chewy sweets. She went in the bathroom, sat on top of the closed toilet seat and stuffed as much of the candy as she could in her mouth, savoring every fistful until her stash was gone.

She leaned back and closed her eyes as the rush flowed through her like an addict's high.

Getting up slowly, she lifted the top of the toilet seat, leaned over and stuck her finger as far down her throat as she could.

Chapter 13

"The Maxwell case is scheduled for eleven," Ruby said as she prepared for her patient. She took a one-size-fits-all set of blue scrubs and two towels from the drawer and placed them on the exam table.

"Hmm," Alex murmured, holding up a set of X-rays to the light.

"Did you take a look at her tests results?"

"Yes." He lowered the X-rays and turned to Ruby.

"And?"

"I don't like what I see. Doesn't make sense. I want her to take a bone density test when she comes in."

"Bone density? At her age?"

"Exactly."

"I'll order the tests. Anything else?"

"Not at the moment."

"Are you sure?" She planted a hand on her hip.

"Meaning?"

"I saw the look that passed between the two of you the last time she was here."

"You're imagining things again," he singsonged.

"I know what I saw Hutch."

"A look?"

"You know what I mean."

"I don't need a babysitter. I need an assistant."

"Don't make the same mistake."

"Humph," he snorted in disgust. "Thought we let that go. Guess not." He tossed the X-rays on the table and stalked out.

Kelly spent the better part of the morning getting ready for her appointment. She took extra care with her face as her sensitive skin tended to erupt whenever she became overanxious—today was a classic example. She awoke to find the beginnings of a pimple on her chin, beneath her left eye on her cheek and one right between her brows.

She peered into the mirror and applied the medicated ointment to the troubled spots hoping to nip them in the bud before they exploded into full-blown volcanoes before the end of the day. Generally she didn't use any makeup, but today she added a splash of mahogany lip gloss to her expressive mouth and put on her one pair of earrings.

As usual her hair was pulled into a tight ponytail at the nape of her neck. It was the one way she found to diminish the fullness of her face.

How many times had she looked in the mirror and wished that she had the face of someone else, someone pretty or at least attractive. Sure she'd been out with guys, but she knew they had no interest in her for her looks, but rather what she may be able to do for them with her connections in sports.

The relationships were all short-lived. Over the past year, she hadn't been out on one single date—more from her own choosing rather than a lack of requests. She felt it was better that way. At least she wouldn't get her hopes up that the guy was actually interested in her and not her name or what she represented. It was a lonely life, more so than she ever let on to anyone. But at least she had the track and running, a time when she felt free, powerful and vibrant. It was there that she shined. She was beautiful, smart. On the track there were no secrets, no shame; only her and the wind.

She looked down at the wrappings around her ankle and lower leg. She would run again. She had to.

"They said this session should last about an hour," David said, holding open the hospital door for her. "I'll be back to pick you up then."

"Thanks." She walked inside and went to the registration desk. "I have an appointment to see Dr. Hutchinson at 11."

"Name?"

"Kelly Maxwell."

The nurse looked up at Kelly and her eyes widened in recognition, a broad smile exposing the tiny gap in her front teeth. "Ms. Maxwell. Oh my." She pressed her hand to her chest. "I'm a big fan of yours."

"Thank you."

The nurse stretched her hand across the desk and placed it on top of Kelly's. She lowered her voice. "Dr. Hutchinson is the best in the country," she said, looking deep into Kelly's eyes. "He'll have you back on the track in no time."

"I hope so."

"Don't you worry." She hit a few keys on the computer, waited a moment and pulled a sheet of paper from the printer. She pushed it across the desk to Kelly. "Just sign your name and you can go in as soon as your name is called."

Kelly swallowed. She looked for familiar words on the paper. Her heart thumped in her chest. David came up behind her, subtly putting his finger where she needed to sign while he spoke to the nurse.

"I've heard great things about this hospital," he said, putting on the charm. "I don't remember seeing you the last time we were here. Work here long?"

"It was probably one of my much needed days off." She laughed lightly. "I've been with the hospital for nearly twenty years."

"You're kidding. You must have come straight out of high school." He leaned on the desk while Kelly signed her name.

The nurse blushed. "If that's a compliment I'll take it."

"It definitely was."

Kelly put the pen down and slid the document back to the nurse.

The nurse tore her eyes away from David to focus on Kelly. "Thank you. It should just be a few minutes. He has a patient. Why don't you relax for a bit? They'll call when they're ready."

Kelly nodded, turned and David guided her to the bench to wait. "You did fine," he whispered.

She glanced at him, offering a tight-lipped smile.

They sat down together.

"I can't depend on you for the rest of my life to read everything for me, David," she said from between her teeth. She glanced quickly around then focused on the blue and white tiled floor.

"Haven't I always been there for you, Kelly?"

"Yes, but—"

"And I always will." He put a hand on her back and gently rubbed. "It's a little late in the program. If the media got wind of this they'd have a field day with you. Not to mention all the documents and contracts that you've signed, which might become null and void. There goes your income. Trust me, it would be a nightmare. That's why I'm here. I'm not going to let you down and I'm not going to let anyone find out. It's our secret. I promised you that years ago. I meant it then and I mean it now."

"It's just that I want to be able to take care of those things myself. There has to be some classes that I can take and no one would find out." She turned pleading eyes on him.

"Now is really not the time to discuss this."

"Ms. Maxwell?" Ruby stood in the doorway to the therapy section of the floor and looked around among the crowd of waiting patients. When she spotted Kelly, she waved her over.

Kelly pushed up on her crutches and stood. "See you later."

"I'll be right here when you're done."

Kelly followed Ruby down the corridor to the therapy room.

"How are you today?"

"Pretty good. Day by day getting better."

"Good."

"Umm, how did the tests come out?"

"Dr. Hutchinson will discuss those with you." She pushed open a door at the end of the corridor and turned left. She led Kelly into the exam room.

"You can get undressed behind that screen. Your top and pants are on the table. I'll be back in a few minutes."

Kelly nodded and went behind the screen. She took off her blouse and put on the buttonless smock top. Sitting on the stool, she loosened the Velcro on the boot and eased it off her leg. Her ankle and halfway up her leg were still discolored. Dark bruising marks were still evident around the incision where the screws had been placed in her ankle. She reached down and gently rubbed.

Gingerly she stood and slowly put weight on her foot. An ache ran up her leg, but it was bearable. She took a step and then another. Her heart pounded along with the throbbing in her ankle. Without the support of the boot, the injury felt more fragile, and it made her terribly afraid. Afraid that one wrong move would send her spiraling into agony. A thin line of perspiration made a trail across her hairline. Using the wall for support, she pressed her hand against it and lowered down to the stool. Her breathing came short and fast as if she'd been running. She tugged in long, calming breaths and unzipped her skirt from the back and wiggled out of it, sliding it over her hips, thighs then down her legs. She kicked it away with her good foot then picked up the oversize pants and put them on just as a knock came on the door.

Alex peeked his head in the door. "Are you decent?"

A hot flush infused her. "Yes." Her voice came out in a thin stream. She heard the door close and quickly tied the drawstring around her narrow waist, just as Alex pushed back the curtain.

"Good morning."

Kelly smiled up at him, her fingers still on the strings. His dark eyes rolled ever so slowly over her until she felt him undressing her. Her hands gradually moved from the strings to travel up her belly, to the center of her chest to rest on the pulse that raced in her throat.

"How are you this morning?" He took one step toward her.

"Pretty good. Looking forward to today."

"All my patients say that until I put them through the

paces. Then they hate me and call me nasty names." He grinned.

Kelly laughed. "I'll try to refrain from name calling."

"And so will I," he teased. He glanced down. "How does it feel without the support?"

"Scary."

"That's only natural. You can put it back on and over the next few weeks we'll work you out of it as the ankle gets stronger."

"Okay."

"When you get it on, come up front and I'll go over the test results." He turned, drew the drapes and walked away.

Moments later Kelly came into the exam room. There was equipment that looked as if it belonged in a spaceship. She couldn't imagine herself using any of it.

"It can be a bit daunting," Alex said, apparently reading her mind. "But it's all for the best. All the machines are hydraulic in nature. So you will never lift or pull more than you are physically able to do, which is much different from weight training and resistance."

Kelly nodded as she walked and looked around.

"But before we get started I wanted to go over your test results. Why don't you have a seat?"

She did as asked and sat in front of him. A small table separated them.

Alex opened a thick folder. "First, your blood count is low. That can be worked with using vitamins and a solid diet. But what concerns me most are the X-rays and MRI."

Kelly sat up straighter in the chair and wrapped her arms around her body, bracing herself for the worst.

"Your break is not healing the way it should by this point. The fracture still appears weak."

"What do you mean not healing the way it should?" Panic found a home in each temple and began to beat.

"It's been six weeks since the accident, correct?"

"Yes, about that."

"In that amount of time, and at your age, the break should be completely knitted together and forming a thickness, which it isn't."

The thoughts ran so hard and fast in her head she couldn't catch them to form any words.

"It could be due to several factors—diet, vitamin deficiency, genetics or a combination of all of that. In the meantime, I want to re-cast that ankle."

"Another cast? Not again."

"This one will be light, fiberglass and only up to your mid-shin. You'll barely feel it."

"So you say," she challenged petulantly.

He chuckled. "That's the spirit. First resistance, then name calling."

Kelly lowered her eyes and smiled.

"And you'll see the nutritionist before you leave today, to get you on a diet program to coordinate with the exercise regime. You need to be sure to follow it to the letter. It's very important. Last but not least a bone density test to see if there is any kind of deterioration in the bone that is making it fragile."

"What if you find…deterioration?"

"It's not all that likely, but possible. Let's deal with it, if we come to that point. I want to be sure to rule out everything. That's all." He paused, studied her concentrated expression. "Are you comfortable with everything I've told you so far? Do you have any questions?"

She looked him right in the eye and when she did, her

breath caught short in her chest. The look of concern and sincerity was so strong and so powerful it totally took her by surprise. It conveyed an immense sense of security and well-being and she instantly sensed that she would be in good hands with Alex Hutchinson. Did he evoke the same kind of response in all his patients or just her? Or was his bedside manner simply Oscar worthy?

His brows arched in question when several moments passed and she hadn't answered him. "Kelly...?

She blinked rapidly. "Oh, um...no I don't have any questions...right now."

"Good." He stood up. "First things first. Let's get the new cast on." He came around the table and helped her to her feet.

She inhaled the clean soap and water scent of him and realized how good that smelled. She swallowed.

"Thank you." She adjusted her crutches beneath her arms and followed him across the hall to the casting room.

"Hey Mark," Alex said to the young man who looked as if he enjoyed playing with paints and putty all day. His royal blue smock was splashed with an array of colors along with large dashes of white from the casting materials. His goggles were dotted with flecks of white along with the blue cap that thankfully covered his ponytailed head.

He glanced up from his latest creation and pushed the goggles up to sit on top of his head.

"Hey Doc. What can I do for you?" He held a teenaged boy's arm and continued covering it in gauze dipped in the paste that would eventually harden.

"I have a patient for you. I need her fiberglassed. Right ankle."

"Sure thing. But it will be a while. The clinic is open today. I have about six in front of her."

"Hmm." He looked around. "You're the only one working today? What happened to Lenny?"

"Yep, just me. Lenny is out sick. You're welcome to do it yourself if you don't want to wait. You still remember how, dontcha?" he teased.

"I made my bones in the casting room," he said, feigning a "goodfellas" accent.

Mark chuckled. "Welcome home, partner. Pull up a seat."

"I think I will." He turned to Kelly. "If you don't mind someone kinda rusty working on you, I'd be happy to fix you up."

"Kinda rusty? You *are* kidding."

"Of course…it's only been about ten years since I put on my last cast."

"What?"

"Don't pay Hutch any attention. He trained me. You have nothing to worry about other than his lousy sense of humor."

"Thanks a lot Mark. I was trying to lull my patient into a sense of insecurity."

"See what I mean?" Mark said drolly.

"Well, now that I've been exposed for the expert that I am, let's get started."

He placed his hand at the center of her back and guided her across the room to a vacant workstation. A comforting heat flowed through her and she actually sighed with pleasure.

"Everything will be fine. I really do know what I'm doing," he said in response to her soft moan.

Her cheeks burned with embarrassment. "I trust you."

Without warning, he scooped her up in his arms as if she were no more than a pillow and gently placed her on the table. Instinctively she'd wrapped her arms around his neck. Their faces were inches apart. She could feel the warmth of his breath brush against her cheek.

"That's what I've been waiting to hear."

Alex worked with quiet precision, his large hands stroking her leg and ankle as he gently applied the gauze and solution to cast her ankle.

Kelly held on to the sides of the table for dear life, sure that if she didn't she would reach out and stroke the soft flow of close cut waves on Alex's head. Shivers ran through her body when the warm pads of his fingertips came in contact with her bare flesh. Could he feel her trembling? Her clit hardened to a stiff nub. And she felt her thighs ease slightly open of their own accord.

"I'll be done in a few more minutes," he said briefly looking up at her. Her face appeared flushed, her back was slightly arched and her eyes were glassy. "Are you feeling okay—in pain?"

He put his hand on her knee and that nearly did her in.

She sucked on her bottom lip with her top teeth and shook her head from side to side as her panties grew more damp with his every touch.

He frowned for a moment. If he didn't know better he'd swear she was getting as hot as he was. It took his good sense, a will of steel, and a potential lawsuit to keep from sliding his hands up her thighs. The muscles were taut, perfect and he knew what they would feel like wrapped around his back locking his body to hers. Oh boy, this was not good. He swallowed hard. Get it together, boy. This woman isn't thinking about you.

"Uh, just a few more minutes."

"Sure," she said on a breath.

"You okay over there, Hutch?" Mark tossed out from

across the room, an equivalent of cold water on the fires of hell. It only made matters smolder.

Alex and Kelly looked at each other simultaneously. *Snap, crackle, pop*. He licked his lips. Her nostrils flared searching for the oxygen he'd sucked out of her lungs. He lowered her leg.

"All done," he muttered then slowly stood, never breaking contact with her gaze, needing to assure himself that he wasn't imagining what he saw in her eyes—his hunger, her want. He cleared his throat, stripped off the latex gloves then tossed them in the trash. "You'll need to wait about a half hour for it to completely set. Hope you like the color. Red suits you." He turned and walked over to Mark, patting him on the shoulder. "If you need some tips from the master, I'm in the directory."

"Still an arrogant SOB," Mark quipped. "We still on for the game on Friday?" he called out as Alex pushed through the swinging doors.

"Wouldn't miss it. You're overdue for a butt whippin' anyway." The door swung shut behind him.

Alex hurried down the busy corridor to his office, his lab coat flapping around him. He needed to catch his breath and figure out where his mind had gone. He opened his door and quickly locked it behind him. He went to his desk, took the key from his ring and unlocked the bottom drawer. A bottle of unopened vodka stared accusingly back at him.

He picked it up. His mouth watered, remembering the numbing effects of the odorless liquid. He turned it around in his hand then set it on the desk. He kept it there for times like this. Times when he needed a kick in the ass to knock him back to reality, a reminder of the dark hole he could fall into if he wasn't on his game. He rocked his jaw back and forth in contemplation. Ruby would have to handle Kelly Maxwell from here on out. It was the only way the both of them would come out of this intact, he reasoned, even as thoughts of Kelly and the feel of her skin made his penis throb and push against the fabric that tried to contain it.

Chapter 14

"So how did it go?" David asked as he held the hospital door open for her to exit.

"Fine."

"That's it? Fine?" He guided her toward the parking lot with his hand at the small of her back.

She shrugged. "What is there to tell? I did some tests, got my ankle recast and…that was it."

He stole a look at her profile as he hit the alarm to disengage the locks on the car doors. "How does it feel?"

"Fine."

"Hmm. Fine is the word of the day," he said.

"Sarcasm doesn't become you."

"And one word answers don't become you."

Kelly opened the car door, turned once to look at him and got in without saying anything else.

David came around the front of the SUV and got in

behind the wheel. He turned on the engine and pressed his foot on the gas letting the car rev to a body vibrating pitch. His jaw clenched. He leaned over and turned on the radio then took off.

They rode for several moments in tense silence.

"Look, I'm sorry, okay. I didn't mean to sound so…"

"Bitchy," he filled in for her.

"Yeah." She chuckled. "Just a little tired that's all."

"You're entitled and forgiven." He glanced down at her ankle as he pulled to a stop at the light. "I thought they only tinted those things for kids."

Kelly grinned. "I think it's kind of fun. Hutch said this kind is much lighter."

"Hutch?"

"Dr. Hutchinson. He put it on."

"I see. Didn't think he was the kind of guy who had the time or inclination for such a lowly task as putting on a cast. I'd think he'd have someone do it for him."

"It was busy. He offered to do it to save time."

David gritted his teeth. The very idea that the good doctor had his hands on her… "That was thoughtful."

"Yes, it was." The memory of that final look they'd shared made her pull in a short breath. She twisted a bit in her seat.

"I thought maybe we could go out to dinner tonight. See a little bit of the city if you're feeling up to it."

She turned to him. "Sounds good."

"I'll get some recommendations from the hotel and make reservations."

Kelly leaned forward and turned up the volume on the radio then angled her head to stare out the passenger side window. She wouldn't see Hutch until Wednesday. She propped up her chin with her palm. That was an eternity.

* * *

Alex strolled into his bathroom and turned on the shower full blast. He was beat and couldn't wait for the blast of hot water to massage his overworked muscles. He'd spent two hard hours in the gym after work in the hope that he could sweat the ache in his groin away. Every time he thought about Kelly Maxwell, a lump formed in his pants. This was crazy. He felt like some inexperienced adolescent who never had none.

He stripped out of his clothes and tossed them in a pile on the black-and-white tiled floor. He stepped over the heap and reached for the shower door, just as his phone rang.

"Damn." He started not to answer but thought it might be the hospital, even though he wasn't on call. If there were any major accidents that required his expertise they would call him in Tahiti if they believed they could fly him back in time.

He reached for a towel to wrap around his waist, but changed his mind. Nobody here but me. So what if his nosy neighbors across the street got a peek. It would give them something else to chat about other than the women who frequented his bachelor pad.

He snatched up the phone in the adjoining bedroom. "Hello?"

"Hey baby."

"Charisse...how are you?" He sat on the side of the bed. He'd met Charisse Clark at a birthday party for Darren Butler, one of his college buddies and closest male friend. Darren had seen to the introductions having prepped Alex in advance that he had the perfect woman for him. Darren had the misconception that since he'd been happily married for the past six years, his goal in life was to marry off all of his friends—with Alex topping the list.

Charisse was great to look at, intelligent, independent—had a great job and was a tigress in bed. A guy couldn't ask for more in his woman, but for Alex something was missing. He simply could not figure out what it was.

"Thinking about you," she was saying.

"Is that right? Good thoughts I hope."

"Always."

"So…what's up?"

"I was fixing dinner and realized that I didn't feel like eating alone. I was hoping to get you over here, feed you, pamper you a little bit and send you on your merry way—in the morning."

Alex smiled slightly. The offer was certainly tempting. The last time he and Charisse spent the night together neither of them got a moment's sleep. He could almost see that dynamite body of hers materialize in front of his eyes.

He frowned and glanced down between his muscled thighs. Not a twitch, not a tingle. Nothing. For a flash he panicked. That had never happened to him before. Never. Even when he'd been stricken by a monster case of the flu, he'd still been raring to go.

"Alex?"

He blinked. "Uh, yeah…" What if he couldn't perform?

"Is that a yes?"

He swallowed, closed his eyes and stroked himself for a moment conjuring up an image of him and Charisse twisting in the sheets. Zip.

"I'm getting a complex over here. If you have something else to do, just say so."

"No, I'm sorry. Listen I don't have anything else to do. I swear to you. I'm just beat. Had a long, rough day. That's all." He hoped that's all it was.

"I could come—"

"Naw, really, babe, I'm beat. I was in surgery for hours. I'm going to hit the sack early. As a matter of fact I was about to step in the shower when your call came." He heard her sigh, hoped he hadn't hurt her feelings. But at the moment a more pressing matter was at hand.

"All right."

"Can a brotha get a rain check?" he teased.

Her tone lightened. "Of course."

"Great. I'll call you…tomorrow," he added quickly.

"Have a good night, Hutch."

"You do the same." He yawned for effect and hung up. He looked down at himself. Not a spark of life. Damn he was too young to be impotent. He hadn't been drinking. He stood and walked to the mirror. This was crazy. He sure hadn't felt like this earlier when he was putting that cast on Kelly's leg.

Twitch. Thump.

"Damn." He glanced down and watched the miracle that was the male sex organ spring to life. *Kelly Maxwell.* He was in real trouble now.

Chapter 15

Kelly studied her meal plan, taking her time to decipher each of the words. Thankfully the relaxing dinner with David and the non-taxing conversation cleared her head. The words weren't scurrying across the page or turning into symbols that she couldn't understand. It was still difficult, a fact that she'd had to deal with all her life. Teachers thought she was stupid and children—who can be such unkind creatures—teased and tormented her relentlessly. No one ever understood how inadequate it made her feel, how lonely she was. To comfort herself she ate…and ate. Food was her friend; at least it had been until she realized that the excess weight she carried around with her hampered her ability to escape the torment of the kids in the neighborhood. Fat and stupid, what a combination.

A gentle knock on her door pulled her away from her

thoughts. She pushed up from the couch and limped over to the door that separated the suites. She opened the door.

"Uh, just wanted to check on you before I turned in." David slid his hands in his pockets.

"Thanks, I'm fine. I was getting ready to turn in."

He looked down at the papers in her hand. "I'll read those to you tomorrow."

"I think I can manage—"

He reached for the papers and took them out of her hand. "We'll go over them in the morning. Don't trouble yourself." He smiled and tucked a loose strand of her hair behind her ear. "Get some rest." He pulled the door close.

For several moments Kelly stood there before locking the door. She turned away and went into her bedroom. Digging through her drawer hidden beneath her lingerie was her second stash.

She pulled out the clear plastic bag filled with sweets. She emptied the contents on the bed and spent the next ten minutes shoving chocolate and chewy candy in her mouth.

"The test results are back," Ruby said, depositing the file on top of Alex's cluttered desk.

He glanced up from the images on the computer screen. "Thanks," he murmured.

Ruby took a seat without asking. "Everything okay?"

"Far as I know," he quipped, giving her a wink.

"Don't you want to know the results of the tests?"

He pushed back a bit from the desk, folded his arms across his chest and pursed his mouth. "You want to tell me, so why don't you?"

Ruby rolled her eyes before speaking. "Ms. Maxwell has some problems."

He sat up a little straighter.

"She has high contents of acid in the urine, her white count is a bit high and there is definite weakening of the bones."

He reached across the table and snatched up the file. "Are you sure?" He frowned as he flipped open the chart and carefully studied the results line by line. The crease between his smooth brows deepened. Slowly he shook his head. "Doesn't make sense. She's what, twenty-nine?"

Ruby nodded. "Same thing I thought."

"How much information do we have on her family history?" He flipped through some more pages, running his finger along the intake information.

"Not much as you can see. She knows nothing about her mother other than her name. Father unknown. Raised by her grandmother who is deceased."

Alex ran his hand across his chin, absently surprised by the stubble. He'd slept badly, tossing and turning most of the night, alternately tormented by accusations of inadequacy from Charisse and uncontrollable desire for Kelly. He'd awakened frustrated and groggy, totally forgetting to shave.

He shut the file and stared at nothing in particular other than the possibilities of deterioration in Kelly that were swimming around in his head.

"What are you thinking?" Ruby interjected.

Slowly he focused on his assistant. "There's obviously something going on here that we need to know about. I don't think it's hereditary."

"Neither do I."

They shared a meaningful glance.

"She's due in tomorrow, right?"

Ruby nodded.

"I'm going to do some reading. I'm hoping it's not what I think."

"But if it is, at least it's treatable."

"Depends on how long she's been bingeing and purging and what the root cause is."

Chapter 16

"Ready?" David asked as Kelly slowly made her way across the smooth wood floors.

"Yep."

"How'd you sleep?"

"Fine. I'll just be happy when I can finally get this thing off my leg."

"Of course you will and so will I." He put his arm around her shoulder and pulled her along the side of his body. "This will all be over soon," he soothed. "Just be patient." He kissed the top of her head. "Come on, let's go."

"Ms. Maxwell," Ruby greeted. "How are you today?"

"Pretty good." She stepped into the treatment room that already had three other patients working out on the various machines. She looked around. "Busy today."

Ruby chuckled. "This is a slow day."

"Um, where's Dr. Hutchinson?"

"He's in surgery this morning. If he's done in time, I'm sure he'll stop in. He wants to talk to you."

Her heart jumped. "Talk to me? About?"

"He'll discuss it with you when he comes in. Why don't you get changed and we can get started."

Kelly nodded, picked up the set of blue scrubs and hopped, walked to the dressing room. Ruby was waiting for her when she got out.

"Let's start with the light machines. You need to build your strength."

An hour and a half later, she was exhausted but strangely exhilarated. She felt good. It had been so long since she'd been able to do anything physical. To her, exercise and running were like drugs. She needed them.

"How are you feeling?" Ruby asked after Kelly returned from changing back into her gray sweat suit.

"Wonderful." She grinned. "Achy a little bit, but in a good way."

"Well, we are going to start slow, let you build your muscles back up without overtaxing them. And a lot will depend on how well and how quickly that ankle continues to heal."

"Good afternoon, ladies."

They both turned at the sound of Alex's voice. He stood in the doorway and took in Kelly with one long look, wondering how a woman could look that tempting in a gray sweatsuit. Inwardly he smiled. He knew because his fertile mind had already imagined what it looked like beneath.

Kelly felt a warm flush move like a gentle massage over her body at the sight of him. This was crazy. She barely knew the man. Maybe it was the white coat—the image of authority. Or maybe it was the glint of something hot and tempting that lingered in his eyes and the corners of his mouth. He was her doctor, nothing more.

He strode into the room, a chart beneath his right arm. "How did it go today?"

"Good," Kelly said. "I think," she added with a smile and turned to Ruby for confirmation.

Ruby nodded in agreement. "She's a good patient."

"If you're all done, I wanted to talk to you for a moment. Go over a few things."

Kelly swallowed. "Okay."

Alex looked briefly around. "No bodyguard today?" The right side of his mouth inched upward mischievously.

"He's in the waiting room—waiting."

"Good. I won't keep you long. Come with me."

"See you on Friday," Ruby said.

Kelly waved goodbye to Ruby, followed Alex out of the treatment room and down the corridor to his office. Every staff member they passed offered a smile or a warm greeting to him. There were even a few shouts and waves from patients. He seemed to be well liked. He opened the door for her and held it as she stepped past him then went in.

Alex closed the door behind him, hurried inside and pulled out a chair for her.

"Thanks."

He held her arm as she sat down, placing her crutches between her legs. When she was settled he walked behind his desk and sat down. He linked his fingers together on the short stack of file folders. He cleared his throat and flipped open her chart to keep from staring at her.

"I wanted to go over your test results and some concerns that I have."

Her eyes widened slightly. "Concerns?"

"Yes. Your family history is very sketchy…pretty much non-existent. Do you remember anything at all about your parents, perhaps something that your grandmother told you."

"No." She glanced away then focused on her long fingers, linked tightly together on her lap.

"Hmm." He rubbed his chin stubble—and was reminded again of another sleepless night. He shifted a bit in his seat. "The reason why I'm asking—"

"There's nothing that I can tell you. My mother was dead before I could even say 'mama.' Didn't know what a father was until I got to first grade." She drew in a breath. "My grandmother only had advice, no information." She stared into his eyes almost daring him to pursue the subject.

"I see." He closed the folder then pressed his lips together in thought. "How is your current diet?"

"What?" Caught off guard by the change in subject her eyes flashed for an instant.

"Your diet. What do you normally eat?"

"I…eat a lot of pasta, um, chicken and fish."

"Are you able to keep it down…when you eat?"

She frowned, glanced away then looked back at him. "That's a silly question."

"I don't think so, Kelly…Ms. Maxwell. There are indications that your body is under severe strain and it's not maintaining the nutrients that it should. Your electrolytes are very low. And for someone your age and apparent good physical condition your bones are weakening."

Her heart thudded, once, twice. The pulse in her neck beat against her skin. "I feel fine."

"Do you?"

"Are we finished? David is waiting for me."

"In order for you to recover you need to be honest with me so that I can put together the best program for you."

"I am being honest. I eat. Don't I look healthy?"

"Looks can be deceiving. Especially when people have become very skilled in hiding their behavior." He gave her a long, meaningful look.

Kelly remained silent.

"I want you to meet with the nutritionist once per week along with your two days here in therapy. She will be monitoring your diet that we've set up. Does that work for you?"

"Do I have a choice?"

"No. Not if you want to get well."

She pushed up on her crutches and stood. "I want to run again. Whatever that takes to make it happen, I'll do it. It's my life." She paused a moment. "What are the chances of that happening?"

He thought of Leigh. She couldn't face not being who she once was and ended her life to end that pain. What would Kelly do if she could not run again? He wouldn't have her on his conscience, too. He reached into his desk and took out a prescription pad and scribbled on it. He handed it to her.

She took it and asked, "What is this?"

"A script for some vitamins and glucosamine for your bones. He stood up then came from behind his desk. "Make sure you take them as directed." He walked to the door and opened it for her. "I'll walk you out."

Kelly got to the door and stopped just as he was opening it. They were very close to each other. She could see the pores in his chocolate brown skin. "You…didn't answer my question." He was so close she held her breath in anticipation—of something.

Alex wanted to tell her that she would be fine, as good as new, better in fact. But he wouldn't make that mistake again.

"I don't know," he said simply.

Her lips tightened. He saw the short intake of breath. She nodded her head and they walked out.

When they arrived at the front desk David was there waiting. He came over to Kelly. "How'd it go?" he asked ignoring Alex.

"Fine."

"What's that?" he asked indicating the paper in her hand with a lift of his chin.

"A prescription for some vitamins."

"I'll take it and get it filled for you."

"I can—"

He took the papers from her hand and gave her a placating smile. "Didn't I say I would handle things? I don't want you to worry about anything except getting better and back on the track." He patted her shoulder. She lowered her head and nodded in compliance.

Alex watched the exchange with interest. The dynamics between the two of them was much more than coach and athlete. David treated Kelly as if she was helpless, unable to think and act on her own without his input and direction. And she treated him with an odd deference.

David looked at Alex. "Anything that I should know?"

"I'm sure Ms. Maxwell can bring you up to speed." He reached into his smock pocket and pulled out a business card then handed it to Kelly. "You call me if you need to," he said, lowering his voice to an intimate level, looking deep in her eyes. He took a second card and gave it to David. "And here's one for you. I don't want you to feel left out." He gave David a smug grin.

David snatched the card and shoved it into his pocket.

"Make sure you eat what's on the plan and take the medicine as prescribed. Take care." He turned and walked down the hall.

Kelly watched as Alex was stopped by a sexy looking nurse with a too short white uniform and dancer's legs, who seemed determined to hold him in place with a hand on his arm. He smiled down at her and she actually batted her eyes. Kelly rolled hers in disgust.

"Come on let's get out of here," David said, stepping into her line of vision.

She accepted the hand on her arm and left the hospital with David close at her side.

While nurse whatshername chatted inanely about something he couldn't care less about, Alex subtly monitored Kelly's departure. It wasn't right whatever it was between those two. It just wasn't right.

David and Kelly stopped off at the pharmacy around the corner from the hotel and had Kelly's prescriptions filled.

David took the three bottles out of the sealed pharmacy bag and read the labels.

"Vitamins and glucosamine. Hmm." He stuck them back in the bag.

"Can I have my stuff, please?" She held out her hand.

He snatched a glance at her. "What's the big deal? I'll give them to you when we get upstairs. I'll explain to you how to take them."

Something let loose inside her. The lid covering the boiling pot shot off and the words came bubbling out.

"I'm not a fucking invalid. I'm not a moron. I'm not a child and I'm not your child! I'm sick of you treating me as if I don't have a thought in my head that's not put in there by you."

His face froze. His mouth opened but no words came out.

Several customers turned in their direction at the outburst.

"You're causing a scene," he said from between his teeth, his eyes darting around at the onlookers. "Lower your voice."

She grabbed the bag from his hand. "If I don't know what they say, I'll figure it out." She turned with as much grace and speed as she could muster and ambled out.

Back in her hotel room, she locked her bedroom door and turned on the music as loud as she could stand it. She wanted to block out David on several fronts.

Staring at her reflection in the dresser's mirror, she saw that the fiery light in her midnight eyes still shone brightly. Her chest rapidly rose and fell. She'd never spoken to David that way. Never. A part of her, the part that clung to his nurturing, deeply regretted her outburst. But this other part, the part that had been dying to be released for so long, was thrilled. She felt as if the doors that had kept her shut in and barred from the rest of the world had been kicked open, setting her free.

She knew that David only wanted what was best for her. She didn't doubt that. But in his desire to do so, he'd put on a choke hold that had been strangling her for years.

It had been so easy to allow him to manage things for her, fix things for her, take care of her. She turned away from the mirror, still unimpressed with what she saw there.

It seemed like she'd been growing up on her own for as long as she could remember. Sure Grandma Stella cooked meals and kept hand-me-down clothes on her back, but that was the extent of any nurturing or offering the kind of love and guidance that a young girl growing up without her parents needed.

When she met David, he was the knight in shining armor, ready to do battle against the world for her. He offered her something she'd never had before—hope and someone who genuinely cared about her. Grandma Stella was more than happy to turn guardianship over to David. Kelly was one less thing she'd have to worry about.

She remembered well the evening he discovered that she couldn't read. They'd been sitting in his living room. He was reading the newspaper and she was pretending to read her history book.

"How's things in school," he'd asked, putting the paper aside and focusing on her.

She shrugged. "Okay, I guess."

"What are you studying so hard?"

"History."

He chuckled. "My favorite subject. So what are you reading about?"

Her gaze jerked in his direction and then away. "Nothing really."

"Nothing?" He laughed again. "Well you've been reading nothing for a mighty long time. Are you stuck on something?"

She shook her head.

"So what's the section about?"

"Nothing." Her voice snapped like a whip. "I'm getting tired. Gonna go to bed."

"Hold on a sec." He reached out and held her wrist as she walked past him. He took the book from her hand and frowned. "I thought you said you were studying history."

"I am."

"This is English lit."

She swallowed. "That's what I meant." She wanted to die. She didn't care what anyone else thought of her—well maybe she did. But what David thought really mattered. She didn't want to disappoint him or for him to be disgusted by her.

"Sit down, sweetheart."

His voice was so gentle, so kind, her legs wobbled as she slowly sat down.

"No matter what you tell me it will stay between you and me." He lifted her head up with a finger beneath her chin. He looked into her eyes. "Tell me what's really going on."

Her mouth trembled. She couldn't. She'd tell him a lie, tell him anything but her shameful truth.

"It's okay." He stroked her shoulder. "Can you read, Kelly?"

Her stomach rose to her throat and she knew she was going to throw up her shame right on his living room floor.

She blinked rapidly to stem the tears that welled in her eyes. "Sometimes," she whispered.

He frowned, confused. "Sometimes? I don't understand."

"Sometimes I can read the words and sometimes I can't. I can't make out the letters."

He was silent and she knew that he was going to get up and throw her stupid ass out.

"But sometimes you can?"

She nodded.

"Does your grandmother know?"

She shrugged. "She thinks I'm dumb, like my teachers and the kids in my class. They all do." She sniffed hard and swiped at her wet eyes with the back of her hand.

"You're not dumb." He put his arm around her and pulled her close, talking softly and gently. "From now on, you can depend on me. Understand?" She nodded against his chest. "First thing is we're gonna get you out of that school. You're a talented athlete and I know we can get you a scholarship to a private high school and then college. You only have a year to go before graduation. And this stays between us. I'll make sure of it," he'd said. "I promise."

He'd kept his promise. More than twelve years had passed and David never breathed a word to anyone. He'd taken care of her every need and kept her secret.

But over the past few months she'd battled with the genie in the bottle. She wanted to let it out. She wanted to be free of the constraints of pretending. She wanted to find a way to be better. She longed to read a novel without battling the words on the page or to pick up a magazine and look at more than the pictures. Just before the accident she'd sent away for some information on dyslexia, and found that there were ways to treat it. The woman she spoke to on the phone said Kelly wouldn't be cured but she could find ways to manage it.

That's all she wanted—a way to manage it. But the more she tried to assert herself, take more control over her life, the more David resisted. And as fate would have it, she needed him now more than ever.

She picked up one of the prescription bottles. *Mega multi-vitamins*. Her mouth flickered. Today was an okay day.

Chapter 17

He finally had a day off, the first in weeks and he planned to take every advantage. The Sunday morning was crisp, clear with just enough warmth in the air to make it pleasant without it becoming uncomfortable. He put on an old pair of sweatpants and a T-shirt, grabbed a book from the three-tiered bookcase and headed out.

Manhattan on any day was always busy, but there was a different vibe, a more contained energy in the bustling city on Sunday. The pedestrians strolled rather than hurried, they peeked in store windows and lingered on corners. They took their time with their meals in the rows of outdoor cafés. Gone were the briefcases and laptop carrying bags, designer pocketbooks and business suits, replaced with department store shopping bags, baby strollers, jogging outfits and a parade of pooches in varying sizes and breeds.

Alex loved it here. Born and raised on One Hundred and

Twentieth Street, he wouldn't trade it in for anyplace else, even though he had the opportunity to travel to many corners of the world. Nothing could compare to home.

He strolled down One Hundred and Tenth Street with the intention of killing a few relaxing hours in Central Park—perhaps down by the lake, he thought as he stopped at a corner kiosk and picked up the Sunday *Times*.

Armed with plenty to read, he crossed Fifth Avenue and entered the park just as he heard his name being called. He looked across a patch of concrete and grass and saw Charisse waving at him. She was walking in his direction.

"Hutch." She leaned forward for a kiss.

"How are you?"

"Pretty good. Thought I'd get out of the house for a while."

"Yeah, me, too."

She looked into his coffee-colored eyes. "Why haven't you called me? Have I done something?"

"No. Don't be silly. You know how busy I can get. I'm sorry. It's been really hectic at the hospital."

She reached out and stroked his jaw. "I don't know why you don't go into private practice. You could cut down on your hours, choose your patients and...we could spend more time together." She smiled.

"Not that easy and it really isn't what I want to do. I like where I am."

She pushed out a breath. "Fine. Anyway, you're here now and so am I." She pressed up closer. "Let's make up for lost time. Spend the day together."

This was not the plan. "Charisse—"

"I'm not taking no for an answer this time, Hutch. You owe me," she added, her voice dropping down to a seductive note. "I have a blanket over there and a few snacks." She took his hand. "Come on," she said with a jerk of her head.

Unable to escape gracefully, he followed her across the grass to her blanket and sat down. He looked at all the stuff she'd brought.

"Are you sure you weren't planning on meeting someone here?" He grinned.

Charisse laughed. Her dimples flashed and he remembered how beautiful she was.

"You know I'm a girl that always comes prepared." She opened the wicker basket and pulled out two clear plastic cups followed by a bottle of white wine. "Would you do the honors?" she asked handing him the bottle.

While Alex opened the bottle, Charisse took out crackers, an assortment of cheeses, bite-size pieces of chicken in a sealed tray, napkins and fancy paper plates.

"Impressive," Alex said, chuckling.

"Help yourself. It's not much but enough to take off the edge and absorb the wine." She held out her glass and Alex obliged her by filling it.

Charisse reclined on the blanket and focused on Alex. "You look good, Hutch," she said, her comment spoken with soft sincerity.

"This old thing," he joked.

"You know what I mean." She tapped him on the knee with her free hand.

"So do you."

She lowered her gaze then looked directly into his eyes. "I...I'm in love with you, Alex."

Something hit him in the chest and he couldn't immediately respond. *Love.*

She emptied her glass then put it down. She sat up, then

sat cross-legged and looked at Alex. She reached for his hands and took them in hers.

"I didn't tell you that because I want you to say the same thing to me. Although I'd love to hear it." A nervous laugh followed. "I told you because I wanted you to know. I wanted you to know that this isn't a game for me." Her eyes roamed over his face. "I think we could do wonderful things together, Alex. I know we could." She took a breath. "But I won't wait for you forever. I can't. So... hopefully, one day soon, you'll be able to say the words and we can take it from there." She held his hands for a moment more, let go and quickly refilled her glass as if to fortify herself.

Alex tossed his wine down his throat. He needed something stronger than this. He had no intention of being in love—in lust sure, but not love. He'd been there, done that. It hurt too bad. Charisse was a wonderful woman and if he would ever consider settling down and being in love, she'd probably fit the bill. Inwardly he shook his head. Not now and probably not ever. He looked across at Charisse who was cutting a slice of cheese for her cracker. It wasn't fair to let her continue to believe that there could be any more between them than what already existed—a good time, great conversation, mind-blowing sex and that was it. Charisse was a decent woman, a wonderful one and she deserved someone who could make her happy and it certainly wasn't Alex Hutchinson.

"Charisse, look—"

"I already know what you're going to say, Hutch. You're not in love with me, you don't want to settle down and waiting on you to change your mind would be pointless." She arched a brow in question. "Right?"

"Yeah, pretty much."

She ran her tongue across her lips. "At least you're honest. That's what I've always admired about you." She paused for a moment. "Can you do something for me?"

"Anything."

"Come home with me…one last time." Her eyes pleaded with him.

"Charisse."

"You know how good we are together." She moved closer and began caressing the inside of his thigh. "You know how I can make you feel…how you make me feel. Then you can walk away. It will be over. I want this final time with you. A memory. That's all. You can give me that can't you?"

He covered her hands to still her fingers and the growing arousal she'd stirred in him.

"That's not a good idea. Think of me what you will, but I'm not into goodbye screws. That's not who I am."

Her aquiline features hardened. She moved back. "I see."

"Do you?"

"I'm not a fool, Hutch. In love maybe, but not a fool." She refilled his cup and then her own. She raised hers. "To old times and bright futures," she said, her voice tremulous but clear.

He touched his glass to hers.

When Alex returned home shortly after, his answering machine light was flashing. He ignored it. He didn't feel like responding and didn't feel like hearing what anyone else had to say.

He tossed his unread book on the bed, followed by the newspaper. He walked into the kitchen, opened the fridge and hunted around the minimal interior, moving half-filled jars and empty containers around hoping something worthwhile would magically materialize.

Coming up empty he shut the door. "The life of a bachelor," he muttered, pulling open one of the kitchen drawers for a menu from one of the local restaurants.

He took out a handful and dumped them on the table. He could easily be sitting in Charisse's apartment, enjoying what he knew would be a delicious meal, followed by stimulating conversation and even more stimulating sex. Instead he was in a sparsely furnished apartment, alone, scouring menus—hungry and horny. Lousy combination.

The phone rang. He pushed away from the table then picked up the wall phone by the sink.

"Hello?"

Silence.

"Hello?"

"I…I'm sorry. Wrong number."

The dial tone hummed in his ear.

He frowned then slowly hung up the phone. Normally he would ignore the call and write it off as a wrong number. But he couldn't. He picked up the phone and dialed *69. The mechanical voice gave him the number of his last incoming call. He dialed and the call was answered on the second ring.

"Good afternoon, this is the Marriott Hotel. How may I direct your call?"

"Uh, I'm sorry, wrong number." He hung up wondering why Kelly Maxwell had called.

Chapter 18

Kelly sat on the side of her bed with the phone still in her hand. That was infantile. She could have said something. But when she heard his voice, she suddenly lost track of the bravado she'd had when she plucked his card from her pocket and dialed the number. She didn't expect him to answer, figured she'd get an answering service.

She returned the phone to its base and silently prayed that he didn't recognize her voice—or maybe that he did.

Ruby was in the training room when Alex walked in.

"Hey boss. How was the weekend?" She continued folding towels and stacking them on the shelves. When she didn't get an immediate answer she turned in his direction. "That good, huh?"

"What?" he asked.

"You're apparently elsewhere this morning. What's up?"

He came fully into the room and pretended to be totally fascinated by the treadmill. "Nothing. Everything's cool."

"Really?" The one word rang of skepticism.

"Yeah, really."

She planted fisted hands on her wide hips. "Told you about lying to me."

"Why do I always have to be lying?"

"Not always, just right now." She put the last stack of towels down on a push-up bench and walked over to him. "You ain't paying that damned machine a bit of attention so stop pretending. What's wrong?"

"Broke up with Charisse this weekend."

Her right brow arched a notch. "You gotta do better than that. I know good and well that wouldn't rock your boat one way or the other. Nice girl and all but she's not for you. Told you that a long time ago. So what's the real story?"

He pushed out a breath. "You're worse than a mosquito."

"So I've been told. Spill it."

He finally faced her and leaned against the bar of the treadmill. "I got a strange call on Sunday."

"And…"

"It was from Kelly Maxwell."

"Oh…I see. What did she want?"

"I have no idea. She didn't say."

"Huh? Then what *did* she say?"

"Nothing. Just that she had the wrong number and hung up."

"She said, 'Hello, this is Kelly Maxwell. Sorry I have the wrong number.' Is that what you're telling me."

"The last part. She didn't tell me who she was."

"Then how do you even know it was her?"

"I recognized her voice."

"Hutch...is there something going on between you two that I ought to know about so that I can kick your handsome ass?" She jerked her neck to the side in a homegirl pose.

"I don't think that would be necessary. Besides you know I could take you in less than five minutes."

"As long as I get a good one in it doesn't matter." She sat down on a stool, rested her arms on her thighs and leaned forward. "I've seen that look in your eyes before and I've watched how you look at her. You don't want to go there. You really don't."

His gaze settled on her face. The concern he saw there was real. She knew what he'd gone through after Leigh's death. She was the one who held his head and put cold rags on his neck when he was sicker than a dog after one of his all-night drinking binges. And he always knew that he couldn't lie to her. She'd never believe him anyway.

"I know it's stupid, but...I'm attracted to her. And it's not that doctor-patient thing. He lowered his gaze for a moment, folded his hands in front of him. "This is different, Ruby. I know I'm walking on shaky ground. But—"

"Will you at least promise me that you will wait until after she's finished here before you try to pursue anything? You don't even know if she feels the same way."

His eyes connected with hers. "She does."

Ruby shook her head more in confusion than annoyance. "She's not even your type. I've seen the kind of women you're attracted to. Kelly Maxwell seems to be nice enough but she's not that cute."

"I think she's beautiful." Even as the words came out of his mouth he was surprised to hear them.

"Hutch..." Her tone singsonged a warning. "Leave her alone."

He blew out a breath. "Yeah, you're right." He pushed away from his resting spot and walked toward the door. "Maybe I should take myself off the case." It was more a question than a statement.

"Her bodyguard would have a fit…as much as he already doesn't like you, I'm pretty sure that wouldn't sit very well with him."

He slung his hands into his pants pockets, pushing aside his lab coat in the process. As usual he was garbed in his faded jeans and a T-shirt, very un-doctorlike but folks around the hospital had gotten used to it, and the chief had grown weary of trying to get Alex to conform. Alex insisted that it made his patients feel more comfortable.

"I'll take your advice into consideration."

"That's wise, as I am." She winked at him. "We have a full day so you need to get your head out of the clouds and into gear."

He opened the door.

"She'll be here today at eleven. Don't forget what I said."

He shot her a parting look and walked out.

"You have to go back?" Kelly asked, a note of alarm lifting her voice.

"I got the call last night. Reggie had a heart attack."

Her hand flew to her mouth. "Oh no. Is he alright?"

"I don't know. He's in the hospital, hasn't regained consciousness as of the phone call from his wife."

She limped over to the couch and slowly sat down then looked up at the worry tensing the space between his brows. "When are you leaving?"

"This afternoon. I know you have a session today. I'll take you to the hospital then I need to head to the airport.

The hotel is paid for and we can arrange for a car service to get you back and forth. I'll turn in the rental van."

She pushed her loose hair away from her face, tucking it behind her ears. "Don't worry about me, okay? I'll be fine."

He came to her and sat down, put his hand on her thigh. "I really hate to leave you alone. I'm the one who got you all the way out here away from everyone and everything and..."

She stopped him. "I'll be fine. I promise."

He heaved a sigh then nodded. "You know the routine with your medications, even if you have a bad day, right?"

"Yes. I know what to do. And you know that as long as I get enough rest and don't get worried about things, I'm pretty okay."

He leaned over and put a light kiss on her forehead. "I'm sorry."

"Don't be." With David gone maybe she would have a chance with Alex...maybe.

Chapter 19

He spotted her the moment she walked through the doors of the hospital and for reasons that escaped him the aggravation of the previous hour, debating with a parent over the proper treatment of her child's broken wrist, suddenly evaporated.

She was listening to David. Her expression was tense but animated as he spoke. No, she wasn't beautiful in the traditional sense, her features were a mixture of this and that and on anyone else it would have been a mess. But put together on Kelly it was an intriguing, natural beauty unadorned by makeup and fancy hairstyles. She put him in the mind of Angela Bassett, strong, flawless complexion, can't be ignored features with an inner energy that forced you to look at her and a smile that lit her up from the inside out.

He slowly put the chart down on the desk when her gaze scanned the crowded room and found him. He would pay

Ruby money on the belief that he'd sworn he saw a glimmer of a smile move her lips. And not the kind of "I'm glad to see my doctor" smile. But an "I'm glad to see you" smile.

They walked toward him. David's usual scowl was in place. Alex ignored it and him.

"Good morning. You're scheduled for eleven." He glanced quickly at the overhead clock. "You're a little early."

"I made the decision to bring her early," David said. "I have a plane to catch."

"Oh, that's too bad."

"What?"

Alex switched his expression of sarcasm to one of concern with a cocking of his brow and tightening of his mouth. "It's too bad that you had to do that. We could have arranged to have an ambulette come and pick her up...is what I meant."

"I wasn't aware of that."

"Will you be gone long?" Hopefully.

"I'm not really sure. However, I'm always accessible by cell phone and Kelly has all of my numbers."

"I'm sure she does." He zeroed in on Kelly. "How are you feeling? Have a good weekend?"

An instant of panic sparked in her eyes. She glanced away, took a quick breath and pushed out a tight no-teeth smile. "Pretty good. Quiet actually," she said while nodding.

"Yeah, me, too." He held on to her with a look before clearing his throat and reluctantly returning his attention to David. "If you speak with the nurse at the registration desk she can get all the information so that Kelly can be picked up and brought back on the days she has a session."

"I'll be sure to take care of it." He didn't move.

"Maybe you should do that now, David. You need to be at the airport in less than an hour and I still have to wait awhile before it's my treatment time." She looked up at Alex. "Do you think the service could take me back to the hotel today?"

"I'm not sure of the schedule on short notice. But the nurse would know. If not, I'll make sure you get home safely." He felt David shift his weight in his direction. "We'll get you a car service. There are plenty that the hospital is affiliated with." Man, he was easy.

"Great." She looked at David. "Maybe it can get set up today," she said suggestively, wondering how long he was going to stand there throwing off nasty vibes. His chest must have puffed up to twice its natural size he was so pissed off. It was plain even to a blind man that these two had no love lost for each other. For the life of her she really couldn't understand what David's problem was. She'd liked guys before. She'd been with her share of men. David knew it. But there was something about Alex Hutchinson that totally rubbed him the wrong way.

David pushed back the cuff of his white shirt and checked his watch. His eyes darted from Alex to Kelly to the nurse's station, calculating the distance and if he would be close enough to hear what was said.

"I'll take care of it." He shot Alex a warning glance.

Alex gave him a stiff, two-finger salute that only pissed David off more. He marched away, albeit with reluctance.

Kelly didn't waste an instant. "Before you say anything, I'm sorry about the phone call. It was silly. I should have said what I called to say."

Her admission caught him off guard. He was certain that they were going to play a game of pretend it didn't happen. But what was more surprising was her expression. It softened, a hint of a flush warmed her cheeks and her eyes widened ever so slightly and Alex knew in that instant what she would look like when he made love to her for the first time—soft, vulnerable and willing.

"What had you intended to say?"

"That I was…thinking about my future, possibly a non-athletic future and I was wondering if you'd ever had a patient like that—someone whose life was totally altered. What did you do, what did they do?"

Leigh's image flashed in his head. He sucked in a shot of air. "I, uh…sure."

"I have everything taken care of," David said, his timing impeccable.

"Great. Well you have a safe trip. Kelly will be perfectly safe with us. And you, Ms. Maxwell, I'll see you in about forty-five minutes." He nodded to them both and walked off down the corridor.

David's jaw was so tight, Kelly could hear his teeth grinding. "Thanks for taking care of that."

He handed her a piece of paper. "Let me go over this quickly." He put his hand on her back and ushered her to a bench out of earshot. They sat down.

"Monday, Wednesday and Friday." He pointed to each word. "The ambulette will pick you up in front of the hotel at ten fifteen. You should wait in the lounge near the exit when you're done. Your name will be called when your driver is here to pick you up between two and three." He glanced at her. "Are you okay with this?"

"Yes. It's very simple. In a couple of days it will be routine. Don't worry." She smiled and patted his shoulder. "I really will be fine, David, and you'll miss your plane if you don't hurry."

He straightened then stood. "You're right. I guess I can get a cab out front." He reached for his traveling bag. "I'll call you this evening."

"Okay. Give Reggie my best. Tell him to hurry up and get well."

"Yeah. I'll call you."

"You told me." She laughed lightly. "Go."

He looked at her one last time, wishing that he was taking her with him and out of the hands of the good doctor. He knew it was silly, this thing he had about the doctor. But in the years that he'd known Kelly and seen her with different men, he'd never felt the least bit threatened by them, never felt that they could ever take her away from him. Alex Hutchinson was a different story and he didn't like it one bit.

"Take care of yourself."

"I will."

David gave a sharp nod and hurried toward the exit. In moments he was swallowed up in the flow of human traffic on the busy circular walk of the hospital and out of Kelly's line of vision.

She glanced down at the paper in front of her. Monday, Wednesday, Friday…simple enough. And now with David gone and not hovering over every move she made, there may be a way to schedule Dr. Hutchinson into her routine. She sat down and waited.

"Ms. Maxwell…"

Kelly looked toward the open doorway and spotted Ruby. She smiled, eased up from her seat and eagerly looked forward to her treatment.

Chapter 20

"How are you today?" Ruby asked once they'd entered the treatment room.

"Pretty good. Getting better day by day."

"Wonderful. And you didn't experience any odd pain or discomfort following your last visit?"

"No."

"And you've been sticking with the diet and the light exercises?"

"Yes, ma'am."

Ruby chuckled. "I'm sorry, honey. I know I can sound like a drill sergeant sometimes, but I want my patients to do well and in a hurry."

Kelly smiled. "I understand and I appreciate it. I really do."

"Okay then, let's get started. You know where everything is. I'll be back to get you started on the weights in about five minutes. I need to check on Mr. Harper on the treadmill. I leave him alone too long he's liable to walk all the way to China."

Kelly laughed, feeling good and hopeful. "Is Dr. Hutchinson coming around?"

"He got called away to an emergency surgery just before you came in. You'll probably see him on Wednesday."

"Oh." She felt as if she were suddenly stooped over, like all the air, the stiffness in her body, had been pulled out. She watched Ruby chastise Mr. Harper and knew that this was going to be the longest two hours of her life. But that didn't stop her from glancing at the door every time it opened on the faint hope that Hutch would walk in.

He didn't.

Kelly went through her rigorous routine of leg lifts, and weight resistance. Ruby was a hard taskmaster and totally ignored grunts and pleas for mercy. The one joy was the sauna followed by a massage that almost made the two hours of torture worth it.

"You need to go on down to X-ray when you get changed. We want an update on that ankle," Ruby said as she massaged Kelly's foot. "It looks good, no discoloration or swelling." Gently she lowered Kelly's leg and straightened up, rubbing the small of her back as she did so. "Whew, not as young as I used to be."

"None of us are."

Both women turned in the direction of Alex's voice. He approached, taking off his surgical cap in the process.

"How'd it go?" he asked.

"I don't know how long I'm going to be considered a good patient," Kelly said and lightly nudged Ruby with her elbow.

"Told you, I'm here to whip you into shape whether you like it or not," she said with a sharp nod of her head.

"Unfortunately she means it," Alex said. He came around Ruby and helped Kelly down from the table. "How does it feel?"

"Wonderful," she said on a breath.

Ruby loudly cleared her throat. "She needs to go over to X-ray."

"I'll take her over." He pulled out a wheelchair from against the wall and opened it. "Your chariot." He gave a mock bow that made Kelly giggle.

"I can take her," Ruby interjected.

"That's fine. I was on my way over there anyway," Alex said.

Ruby shot him a look of warning.

"See you later."

He pushed Kelly out of the room and into the corridor.

"Ruby can be kind of tough sometimes, but she means well," Alex said while pushing her down the hallway.

"I know. I don't mind, really."

"How are you feeling today?"

"Pretty good."

"Was David able to get you squared away for the hospital transport service?"

"Yes, they'll pick me up when I'm done. I have to let the nurse up front know when I'm ready."

"Uh…I can take you today. I'm off in an hour."

Her heart knocked in her chest. "Well…if you're sure and it's not taking you out of the way."

"It's really not a problem."

A fire ignited in her stomach, fanning outward to her limbs then straight to her head. "Sure. Fine."

"It's done then. I'll meet you up front when my shift ends. If I run into any trouble, I'll let you know."

She nodded her head, uncertain of her voice.

"Here you are." He pulled the wheelchair to a stop. "Steve, this is Ms. Maxwell. He pulled her chart from the back pocket of the wheelchair. X-ray of the right ankle." He handed the radiologist the chart.

"Sure thing. I have one ahead of her." He looked down at Kelly. "You can wait right over there," he said pointing to a row of chairs along the light green wall. "The nurse will call you when we're ready for you."

"Page me when she's done, Steve."

"Sure thing."

"See you in a few," he said to Kelly before turning and walking away.

Kelly, finished with her X-ray, waited near the entrance trying not to look as anxious as she felt whenever she saw a tall, brown-skinned man in a white coat approach. But she didn't realize just how much she wanted to see Alex until he actually appeared in front of her. Was she smiling in response to his? She couldn't tell. All she knew was that for the first time in ages, she felt excited about something other than the next race.

"Sorry to keep you waiting. I had a consult."

"Not a problem."

He helped her up and held her arm while she adjusted the crutches.

"I'm out in the parking lot."

They walked out in silence, but Kelly's pulse was beating so loudly in her ears she wouldn't have heard anything he said anyway.

The three sharp chirps of the alarm disengaging on the silver Maxima snapped her out of her daydreaming.

He opened her door and helped her in and she thought that a simple touch had never felt so good and he'd been touching her all day. Innocent touches but touches that set her on fire, making her want more.

"You need more room, you can adjust the seat. The lever is underneath you in the center." He turned the key in the ignition.

"I'm fine."

You certainly are, he thought but didn't say and had an overwhelming urge to touch the silk of her hair, tuck the loose strands behind her ear so that he could better see her profile.

"Hungry? We can stop somewhere along the way."

She was much too nervous to eat. And if she did she didn't want to mar the beauty of her day with one of her episodes.

"I'm fine. Thanks for asking." She linked and unlinked her fingers on her lap, concentrating very hard on the process. It was much easier than looking at Alex. The warm, clean scent of him drifted to her much as sleep sneaks up on you and carries you away. She inhaled slow and deep. Inside she smiled.

"So tell me about yourself," Alex said, pulling to a stop and turning on the right signal light.

"I pretty much told you everything. Not much to tell."

"Of course there is. What's the secret that the papers haven't picked up on, some laundry that's stuffed in the closet?"

"What do you mean?" she asked, the hitch in her voice in concert with the wave that ran through her stomach.

Alex snatched a quick glance at her before making the turn. He frowned in surprise. "Only kidding."

"I'm sorry. I didn't mean to snap. It's just that when you are out in the public eye, you get raked over the coals so often...."

"I can imagine. It must be hard to always be under the spotlight."

"It can be. Especially just before and after major competition. Then there are the hounds that follow you around 'just because.'" She snorted in annoyance.

"How do you manage?"

She shrugged lightly. "David protects us as much as possible. You try to live your life as best as you can so that when they do write something about you it's not as ugly as it could be."

"Do you have fans that stop you and ask for autographs?"

She giggled. "Not as much as basketball and baseball stars, but I get my share. Especially back home."

"Do you go out a lot? I mean in the evenings," he hedged.

"Not really. I go out every now and then." She stopped, turned to him and the question was out of her mouth before she could stop it. "Are you seeing anyone?"

The car jerked forward when he pressed a little too hard on the gas. "Uh, no I'm not. Are you?"

"No."

"You think that's a good thing?"

"That I'm not seeing anyone?" she asked, her voice a bit tremulous.

"No, that neither of us are seeing anyone."

They both looked at each other and smiles of relief and invitation played around their mouths and put a new light in their eyes that popped back and forth between them.

She wanted to touch him. Run her finger along the tiny scar above his left brow. Her chest rose and fell slowly and seductively as she drew in deep breaths in the hopes of controlling her rapidly racing heartbeat.

Alex was transfixed by the pulse that raced at the base of her throat, the way her lips trembled ever so slightly and the way her full breasts rose toward him daring him to reach out and caress them.

The blare of a car horn behind them jerked them back in their seats.

Alex sputtered a nervous chuckle. "Causing a traffic jam," he said, pressing down on the gas and zipping through the intersection.

They were quiet for the next few blocks, both contemplating the implications of what they'd revealed. Shortly they arrived in front of the hotel.

Alex eased the car to a stop, turned and looked at Kelly. "Safe and sound." He gave her a half smile, his gaze sheltering the question that danced on his tongue.

"Thanks. I'm sure I can't expect this kind of treatment every day."

"You never know. I don't mind, really, as long as I'm available."

She didn't want to hope. "I'll keep that in mind." She studied her hands for a moment before reaching for the door handle.

"I'll help you." Alex hopped out of the car and came around to her side. He held out his hand.

Kelly stretched out her hand and gently placed it in Alex's. His fingers closed around hers and her insides shifted from left to right as her breath stopped short in her throat. His intense gaze locked onto her and she couldn't seem to move or hear anything around her above the rapid racing of her heart.

Alex stepped closer, leaned inside the car and placed his other hand around her waist. "Easy does it," he said easing her to her feet. He kept his arm around her waist, savoring the moment, the feel of her so close to him.

When she stepped down their bodies were inches apart. Her face was turned upward toward his, her lips slightly parted. She could feel the warmth of him surround her and for a silly moment she wondered if to the casual passerby they looked like models for the cover of a romance novel.

"You're beautiful," he heard himself say and instantly wished that he hadn't. The stunned look on her face rocked him back to earth.

"No one has ever said that to me," she managed to stutter.

"I can't believe that."

She lowered her eyes. "Believe it. Can you pass me my crutches?"

Alex shook himself out of his trance and opened the back door to the car, pulled out her crutches and handed them to her.

"Thanks." She adjusted them beneath her arms, paused, wanting the moments to last, needing to find a way to make him stay. "Do you have to go back to the hospital?"

"No. I'm actually finished for the day. Unless an emergency comes up, I'm free." He waited. Hoped. She had to make the move.

"Why don't you come up for a little while? The least I can do is order room service to thank you for bringing me back."

A crooked grin crinkled the corners of his eyes. "A woman who knows how to tease a man...with food."

Kelly laughed. "Is that all it takes? You're easy." She moved away and went toward the entrance.

Alex gave the keys to the valet and followed her inside.

Chapter 21

Standing next to Alex in the close quarters of the elevator made her light-headed, her knees wobbly and her heart race a mile a minute. She was taking this man up to an empty suite. Just the two of them. She was no naive fool. She knew what that said without the words. It was an invitation to more than "ordering room service," and Alex had accepted.

The bell dinged on the penthouse floor and opened directly onto the spacious suite, offering an immediate panoramic view of the Manhattan skyline. Today the sun's rays glistened against the glass and chrome skyscrapers making them appear like futuristic images on the vast landscape of steel and concrete.

"Impressive," Alex uttered, stepping inside. He turned to Kelly and grinned. "I've been hanging out with the wrong crowd. Do you always travel in this kind of style?"

"We get treated pretty well," she admitted a bit hesitant

on divulging the sometime extravagant settings she'd inhabited during tours and track meets. The athletes were always treated like rock stars, getting the best rooms at the hotels, the best food and service—all generally provided for by very generous sponsors. It was a life to which she'd grown very accustomed.

"Make yourself comfortable. Can I get you anything to drink?" She quickly unplugged the phone while Alex was enjoying the view. The last thing she wanted was to be disturbed by a call from David, which she knew would be forthcoming.

"I'm good." He turned to face her. "Why don't you show me where everything is."

She swallowed. "Okay." She led him toward the small but well-stocked kitchenette. "We generally use room service but if we ever want to do our own thing we can. There's a small fridge, microwave, and dishwasher." She turned slowly. "Down the hall is the guest bathroom." She led him in that direction. "Through those doors is the adjoining suite...where David was. And over there is my room," she said, pointing to the closed door on the opposite side of the living room.

Alex nodded his approval. "Very nice. Almost like home."

Kelly chuckled. "Not in the least. As much as I've traveled, Atlanta will always be home for me."

He sat on the couch and Kelly took a seat on the armchair opposite him.

"You've never considered relocating?"

She shook her head. "No. Atlanta has been good to me," she said, her tone thoughtful. Gone were the frightening days of hunger, torment and loneliness. David made sure of that. No she'd never leave.

"So..." Alex said on a breath. "What else do you like to do besides run like the wind?"

For a moment she frowned. "Not much." She laughed a nervous chuckle. "If I'm not running, I'm in training. When I'm not training I'm sleeping." She stole a glance to gauge his expression but couldn't read him.

"Pretty regimented life. Don't you ever want to go to concerts, plays, go out dancing?" he asked, his voice gentle but probing.

She shrugged and looked away, stretching her injured foot out in front of her. "I don't really think about it much." That was a lie. She often wondered what it would be like to go out on a real date with no strings, to be wined and dined, not have to concern herself with her weight or who was going to snap her picture and make up a story to go with it.

"Well, you know the old saying, all work and no play." He leaned back to get more comfortable and crossed his right ankle over his left thigh. "Playing rounds out your life." He grinned.

"Is that right?" She smiled. "What do you do when you play?"

"Sports are definitely a top priority with me. I have season passes to all the Knicks games...even though they leave a lot to be desired. I attend the US Open like a religion. Jazz festivals, R&B concerts, gallery openings. I try to keep busy otherwise my job will consume me."

"How do you find the time?" she asked really needing to know.

"I make the time. You should, too."

Slowly she shook her head as she spoke. "I don't know. I—"

"Does David allow you to go out?"

Her gaze snapped in his direction. "What's that supposed to mean?"

"Does he have a say so about your activities off the track?"

Her lips pinched. "No. But he wants to make sure we're always prepared. Being an athlete is different. We're not like everyone else."

Alex frowned. "Different? Your blood is red. You put your pants on one leg at a time—"

"Is that supposed to be funny?" she asked, offended by his sarcasm.

"Actually, no. The first part of being an athlete, or any profession for that matter, is being human and kind to yourself. Yes, you have a God given skill, but you are still a woman, with hopes, dreams, needs."

She snapped her head away from looking at him. "You don't understand. David—"

"David controls your life. David tells you how to live, what to do, say, how to act."

"He only wants to protect me," she cried.

"From what?"

"From…"

"Life. Life, Kelly," he insisted. "As long as David can control your every move, your every thought, he can keep you tied to him, beholden to him. He maintains the power and you remain powerless."

She wished she could jump up and run away. Get away from Alex and his conclusions that were too close to the truth. She couldn't let him know the real reason why she was so tied to David, why she needed him.

"Wow, I got you up here on the pretext of fixing you something to eat and I haven't even gotten you a glass of water." She pushed herself up.

Alex was immediately at her side. "Don't run away." He held her by the wrist.

She turned, glanced up at him. His gaze was too intent. "I'm not." She sputtered a nervous laugh. "I can't—remember?"

"You know that's not what I mean."

"Do you want ice in that glass of water?"

He released her and stepped back. "Yeah, ice would be great."

She limped off to the kitchenette. Alex was right behind her.

"You're really good at changing subjects. Obviously it's something you don't want to discuss. I'll respect that and leave it alone."

She lowered her head while pouring him a glass of water from the carafe. "Thank you."

She reached in the freezer and took out the ice tray, popped two cubes into the glass and put the tray away. She turned and handed the glass to him.

"I'm really not the enemy."

She didn't respond.

He took a long swallow from his glass while studying her. "Do you think that I am?"

"No."

"Then that's a start. So," he said on a breath. "What's to eat?" He grinned and so did she.

Alex helped her fix a Caesar salad and all the while he couldn't help but wonder what she was so afraid of. It was obvious that she was hiding something. And he was certain it had something to do with her and her relationship with David Livingston.

The knock on the door interrupted their quiet camaraderie.

"Excuse me for a minute. The plates are in that small cabinet," she said. "We can eat in the living room," she added heading to the next room to answer the door, momentarily thankful to put a little space between them.

Alex strained to hear what she was saying, but couldn't. She returned shortly.

"Everything okay?"

She nodded. "Yes, just the front desk wanting to know if I needed anything," she lied.

Alex smiled. "I have been hanging out with the wrong crowd."

Chapter 22

Charisse stood in front of her window looking down on Manhattan from the fifteenth floor of her high-rise apartment building. She sighed deeply. She should have never revealed her true feelings to Alex. She took a sip from her glass of wine. He was everything she wanted in a man, but it was obvious that she wasn't what he wanted. She finished off her drink, walked over to the bar on the far side of the sunken living room and refilled her glass. What was she going to do now? She should have waited, waited until it was too late.

Her phone rang. She thought about not answering but changed her mind. She could use someone to talk to. She picked up the phone from the center of the smoked glass table.

"Hello?"

"Hey cuz."

"Steph?"

"Who else."

Charisse smiled, rested the phone between her ear and shoulder and plopped down on the couch. Stephanie Daniels was her aunt Nell's daughter, her mother's sister. They'd been close since they were kids growing up in the Marcy projects in Brooklyn's do-or-die Bed-Stuy. Both of them had battled their way out of the drug and crime infested neighborhood—Stephanie through athletics and Charisse with her flair for mathematics was now an engineer for IBM.

"I'm sure glad you called, girl. I could use a friendly voice." Stephanie was the sister Charisse never had. She shared much of her life with Stephanie, mostly by phone because of the geographic distance. But they talked often, keeping each other pretty much up-to-date on their lives.

"What's up? You don't sound good. Did you tell him? Did he flip?"

Charisse heaved a deep sigh. "I told him part of it, not everything," she said, sounding like a frightened child instead of a thirty-two-year-old woman.

"What part did you tell him?"

"That I was in love with him."

"Dayum. Wrong confession."

"Apparently."

"What do you mean apparently?"

"He...broke it off."

"Shit."

"My sentiments exactly. What do I do now?" Tears of regret and hurt welled in her eyes and spilled over.

"Well, you have three choices, cuz—tell him and see if he wants to man up and do the right thing, pay a visit to your local clinic or join the ranks of single-motherhood."

Charisse released a slow, silent breath. Whatever she decided, it would have to be soon.

* * *

The moment David landed in Atlanta he pulled out his cell phone and called Kelly. No answer. He tried three times as he exited onto the street and hailed a cab. With each empty ring his frustration level escalated.

He tossed his overnight bag in the back seat, slammed the door behind him. He gave the driver instructions to his town house.

Frowning, he scrolled through the numbers locked into his phone and called the hospital.

"This is David Livingston. I'm calling to find out whether or not a patient, Kelly Maxwell, got on the hospital transport van after her treatment today."

"Are you a relative sir?"

"I'm her coach."

The nurse huffed a bit on the other end. "The vans finished up for the day hours ago, sir. The drivers are all gone. I would have no way of knowing. I only came on duty at four o'clock."

"Is there anyone around who would know? What about Dr. Hutchinson? He's her doctor."

"Dr. Hutchinson is gone for the day. He's been off duty for hours."

David felt as if he would burst. "Thank you…for nothing!" He disconnected the call.

This time he dialed the hotel directly.

"Marriott, may I help you?"

"Yes, this is Mr. Livingston in the penthouse."

"Yes, Mr. Livingston, how can we help you this evening."

"I've been trying to reach Ms. Maxwell but I'm not getting an answer. Could you please try the room? I'm a little worried."

"If I'm not mistaken, I saw Ms. Maxwell go upstairs

quite some time ago. I don't believe she's gone out. Would you like me to try the room?"

"Yes, please..."

David listened to the phone ring and ring.

"I'm sorry, sir, there's no answer."

"Look, I need you to go up to the room. Check and make sure that Ms. Maxwell is all right."

"I'll send someone up right away."

"Thank you."

"Is there a number where I can call you back?"

"I'd prefer to hold on."

The cab stopped in front of his building. Absently he reached into his jacket for his wallet, pulled out a twenty and a ten and handed them to the driver. "Keep the change." He snatched his bag from the seat and got out, walking hard toward his front door, his ear pressed to the phone.

He opened his front door and stepped into a blast of contained heat. Immediately he turned on the air conditioner followed by the ceiling fan. He paced beneath the fan, waiting, listening to recorded music and short spiels about the wonders of the Marriott Hotel.

"Mr. Livingston..."

David snapped to attention. "Yes."

"Uh, Ms. Maxwell said that she would call you, but to let you know that everything is fine."

David frowned. "What? Did you see her?"

"No sir, actually I spoke to her at the door. She sounded fine. Will there be anything else?"

Totally bewildered, he mumbled no and disconnected the call.

What was going on and how much did Dr. Hutchinson have to do with it?

Chapter 23

"The food was great, your choice of music was on point and the company couldn't have been better," Alex said, standing and stretching. "As much as I don't want to I need to head home."

"Thanks for everything. I had a nice time, too." She started to get up. "I'll get your jacket."

He held up his hand. "No. Don't. I'll get it." He lifted his chin in the direction of the hallway off the kitchen. "It's in that closet in back, right?"

She nodded.

"Be right back." He walked down the short hallway and pulled open the closet. When he reached for his jacket he noticed a pamphlet sticking out of one of the other jacket pockets and it immediately caught his attention. He took a quick glance over his shoulder before lifting the pamphlet out. "You and Dyslexia. How to Cope." Slowly he shook his head. Now everything made sense. He stuck the pamphlet back in the pocket and closed the door.

When he returned to the living room, Kelly was still seated on the couch with her head back against the cushions, her eyes closed and her right hand tapping out a beat to the sounds of Kirk Whalum on saxophone.

"He's coming to town in a couple of weeks. Would you like to see him?"

She jerked for a moment, sat up and turned to him. "You...are you asking me out?"

"Yeah, I think so." He chuckled. "Like I said, all work..."

"Well...I..."

"Think about it. The concert is in two weeks. Let me know."

She nodded.

"So I'll see you day after tomorrow. Don't forget to stick with the menu and the vitamins. Very important."

"Sure."

"And thanks again." He walked to the door, turned once. "Take care of yourself."

"You, too."

The door closed softly behind him.

Kelly let out a long breath. He'd asked her out on a date. A slow, steady smile moved across her mouth. He'd actually asked her out. Hopefully David would stay gone for a while. The thought of David made her remember about the unplugged phone.

After reconnecting the phone, she did what she'd been dreading. She called David in Atlanta. He answered on the second ring.

"Kelly? Where the hell have you been? I've been worried sick. Why didn't you answer the phone? What took you so long to call back? I sent the desk clerk up there hours ago."

She could almost see him pacing as he fired questions at her.

"David I'm fine. I turned the phone off so that I could get some rest."

"That's not a very wise thing to do. What if something happened?"

"Nothing happened. I told you I'm fine. How was your flight?"

He pushed out an exasperated breath. "Fine. Long. But I'm here now."

"Any word on Reggie?"

"He's not doing well. He's slipped into a coma."

"Oh my God. Please send my prayers to his family."

"I will."

"What are you going to do?"

"I don't have much choice. I have to stay. The team needs me and I want to be here for Reg. But I want to be there for you, too. You're the one I'm worried about."

"David, please, just take care of things in Atlanta. I'll be fine. I promise. How's everything with the team?"

"I'll see everyone tomorrow at practice. I've called a special meeting. And I'll have to start scouting for an assistant coach as well."

"Hmm."

"How did everything go today?"

"Fine."

"Did the ambulette take you back to the hotel?"

She hesitated for a moment. "Yes. Right on time. No problems."

"Good. Okay, well now that I know you're all right I can relax."

Kelly laughed. "Yes, please do."

"I don't think you realize how much you mean to me, Kelly."

Her breath caught at the sudden intimate tone in his voice. "Of course I know," she said on a light note hoping that she was only imagining things. "I'm your star athlete and you want me to be well and back on the track. And I want to get back out there, too."

Silence hung between them for a moment.

"Get some rest, Kelly. I'll talk to you tomorrow."

"Yes, I will. Take care, David. Good night." She hung up.

David paced his bedroom floor with the disconnected phone still in his hand. The moment those words were out of his mouth, he regretted them. He could tell by Kelly's hesitation and her response that she was put off by what he'd inadvertently confessed.

"Dammit." He tossed the phone across the room where it landed on the couch. He was losing perspective. Having her so close during their time at the hotel had worked on him more than he'd let on. And his feelings only seemed to intensify with the insertion of the good doctor into their lives. He had to get it together. There was a championship at stake. The amount of notoriety and sponsorship dollars he could garner if he pulled out the winning team would make all of his dreams come true. Then and only then would he pursue Kelly the way he wanted.

Kelly was floating. For the first time in weeks she was actually looking forward to the next day and the one after it. She and Alex were going out on an official date. David wouldn't be back anytime soon and she could have some breathing room.

She went to the closet and took the pamphlet out that she'd hidden in her coat pocket. Alex's words came back to her: *as long as David has power over you, you are powerless.* She wasn't going to be powerless any longer. It was time that she finally took control of her own life.

She brought the pamphlet to the living room and sat down. Taking her time she went through the information again. Excitement bloomed inside her. Tomorrow morning she was going to call and make an appointment to go in and speak with a representative. She sat back and smiled. Yes, she was going to start taking control of her life.

Chapter 24

"I called this meeting today to bring everyone up-to-date on what's happening with Reggie and ultimately the team." David cleared his throat and looked around at all the anxious faces. "I spoke with Reggie's wife yesterday when I arrived. Reggie has slipped into a coma."

A gasp circled the room.

"The doctors are hopeful that he will come out of it on his own. But they don't know when or what shape he will be in when he does." He got up from the edge of the desk and stood. "I am going to be looking at a few candidates in the next couple of weeks for a replacement for Reggie. A temporary replacement," he quickly added. "Until then, practice goes on as usual. I'll be here running things and taking care of the day-to-day operations."

"What about Kelly?" Stephanie asked. "When is she coming back?"

David cut his eyes in her direction. "Kelly is going through rehab. When she returns she will be good as new."

"When?" Stephanie pressed. "We have preliminaries in two months."

"I know that," he snapped.

Stephanie folded her arms beneath her breasts. "I think the team deserves to know where we stand and how we are going to handle the prelims," she said sweetly.

"And we will handle it—as I see fit." He glanced around the cramped room. "Any other questions?" It was more of a challenge than a question. "Good. See you out on the field in a half hour."

One by one they filed out, murmuring to each other. David couldn't worry himself about what they thought. His main concern was shaping up a winning team. He knew the whole interpersonal thing was more Reggie's ball game. He was the one who coddled them and served as counselor and father to many. David had always focused on training, the media and the business end of things. And it had worked. Until now. He heaved a sigh.

Stephanie walked out onto the track with an extra bounce in her step. She felt invincible. She knew that, very soon, David would have no choice but to put her at the head of the women's track division. She was faster than ever, could take the hurdles with her eyes closed and it was only a matter of time before she broke precious Kelly's sprinting record. And when she did whatever reservations David may have had would be moot. She would be in and Kelly would be out. Simple as that. The way it was supposed to be.

She gently massaged the tender spot on her upper thigh and smiled.

* * *

David stood along the side of the track while the men's relay team hit the field. He held his stopwatch in his hand as they sped around the track.

"How's it going?"

David turned right, toward the direction of the voice and frowned in annoyance. "What do you want, Miller? This is a closed session."

"I'm a sports reporter, reporting on sports," he tossed back.

"You need to leave before I have security throw you out."

"Answer this for me? Where is your golden girl and when will she be back? Sports fans want to know."

"I won't tell you again. Get out. Now."

"Fine. If you won't tell me, I guess I will have to do my own digging to find out." He turned to leave.

"Wait."

Miller turned back with a smug smile on his face.

"She'll be back on the track in a month. Six weeks at the outside."

Miller arched a brow. "Really, just in time for preliminaries." He made some notes on his pad. "How does Stephanie Daniels feel about that?"

"She's happy. Just like the rest of the team. You have your story so beat it."

Miller grinned. "Thanks for your time." He walked away.

David watched Miller until he was off the training grounds and out of sight. He was a royal pain. Called himself a reporter, but all he wanted to report was sleaze and scandal. David shook his head then turned his attention back to the team. Stephanie was on the starting blocks. He leaned against the fence and checked his watch as she took off around the track.

She didn't have the same smooth form as Kelly but she did have speed. He checked the watch. His eyes widened. He looked out at her again as she flew around the track. She was going to beat Kelly's time. His pulse raced. She was coming into the home stretch. He stepped closer, checked the watch just as she crossed the finish line.

She'd beaten Kelly's record by two tenths of a second. But could she do it again, in competition? Maybe he could win it without Kelly.

"Stephanie!" He waved her over. She jogged to him barely winded.

"Yes, coach?"

"That was pretty good."

She smiled. "I know."

"Let's talk in my office."

"Sure."

"Close the door," David said once they'd reached his office.

Stephanie shut the door then took a seat.

"What is said in here stays here. Is that understood?"

She nodded.

"There may be a possibility that Kelly won't be ready in time for the preliminaries. And I emphasize a possibility."

"And?"

"I want you to be ready to step in."

A slow smile crept across her mouth. "Of course. I'm ready now."

"We'll see. I want to work out a special training schedule for you, starting tomorrow morning. Meet me here at six a.m. sharp."

"I'll be here." She stood. "Thanks for giving me a shot, coach. I won't disappoint you."

"Stephanie, if you breathe one word of this…"

"I won't."

"Good. See you in the morning."

Stephanie headed back to the locker room. Finally, her dreams of stardom were within her grasp. She wouldn't be second fiddle anymore. And before she was done, Kelly Maxwell would barely be a memory.

Chapter 25

Kelly pulled her baseball cap farther down over her brow. She avoided eye contact with the three others in the waiting room on the off chance that someone would recognize her. The longer she waited the more she was beginning to have second thoughts.

"Ms. Maxwell?"

Kelly's heart thudded. She snatched up her purse and limped to the reception desk.

"Ms. Stevens will see you now. It's the second door on the right."

"Thank you." She went down the hall and knocked on the door.

"Come right in."

Kelly slowly opened the door. This was her first big step toward freedom. She shut the door behind her and with it—the past.

* * *

She'd spent more than an hour with Ms. Stevens, answering questions and taking evaluation tests. The conclusion: she was definitely dyslexic, not stupid and there were ways to combat it so that she could actually read and comprehend what she saw on the page. Her particular problem manifested itself whenever she felt stressed and was overly tired. The result was not that she saw letters backwards as many with the learning disability did, but rather she was often unable to process what she saw and the anxiety of it caused the letters on the page to literally move in front of her eyes or what she would write made absolutely no sense to those who read it, though in her mind's eye it was fine.

Ms. Stevens wanted her to attend some relaxation classes once per week and she would be retaught how to think and translate what she saw and read.

"It's not going to be easy," Ms. Stevens had said. "There are going to be days when you will want to give up. But the key to success is your understanding that there will be days when you will be unable to read and when that happens you need to relax, take a break and come back to it later."

"I have a problem with numbers, too," Kelly had said. "Sometimes I get them mixed up. I can't even manage a bank account."

Ms. Stevens gave her an encouraging smile. "You'll learn how to manage that as well. Be patient. I know it has been a lifelong struggle, but you've taken a major step in coming here. Your life is about to change and that's exciting."

Kelly felt encouraged, better than she'd felt in longer than she could recall. She would be able to go into a restaurant and order from the menu not from memory. She'd be able to walk into a bank and open an account and maintain it herself. She'd be able to read a newspaper, magazine or a book and understand what she read. Yes, there would be bad days, but the good days would finally surpass them.

As she rode back to the hotel, clutching the booklets that Ms. Stevens had given her, she was filled with a sense of power. Something she only felt on the track. Now she would have power over her life, and the hold that David had over her would finally begin to loosen its grip.

As soon as she walked into the door of her hotel suite the phone was ringing. Even before she picked it up she knew who it would be.

"Hello, David."

"How did you know it was me?"

"Lucky guess."

"How are you? I called earlier and didn't get an answer. Is everything all right?"

"Everything is fine. I, uh, went out for a walk. I just came in."

"For a walk? Alone!"

"Yes, alone," she said trying to keep the exasperation out of her voice. "I needed some air and the walk is good exercise."

"I really don't like the idea of you wandering around New York alone."

"David, please. I'm not a child! I'm perfectly capable of taking care of myself."

"New York is not back home, Kelly. People there don't care that you're on crutches. They'd just as soon knock you down to get to a bus as steal your purse."

"Yes, it's a real jungle," she said drolly.

"I'm only thinking of your safety."

She didn't respond.

"Did you take your vitamins?"

"Yes." She rolled her eyes. "And I even brushed my teeth this morning. All by myself."

"Sarcasm doesn't become you, Kelly."

"You don't give me much choice. Listen, I don't want to argue. I'm tired. I'm going to take a nap. How is Reggie?"

"Still the same."

"I'm sorry."

"I'll keep you posted. Get some rest. I'll call you later this evening."

"Sure. Bye, David."

When she hung up the phone she really was tired. Dueling it out with David was exhausting. The sooner she got totally out from under his thumb the better off she would be.

David slowly hung up the phone and stared off into space. He didn't like it. He didn't like it one bit. Something was going on with Kelly. Her entire attitude toward him had changed dramatically since she'd been in New York. She'd never openly challenged him and the decisions he made on her behalf. Now, everything was a battle. She had an opinion and an attitude to go with it.

The sooner he got her out of there and back home, the sooner things would return to normal and the old Kelly would return. It couldn't happen soon enough for him.

He sighed. In the meantime, he still needed to find an assistant coach. There were a few really good candidates and he would have to make his decision soon so that he could get back to New York and see exactly what was going on. But he had to be assured that the team would be in good hands during his absence.

He flipped open a folder on his desk of one of the candidates, and was going over his credentials, when there was a knock on his door. He closed the folder.

"Come in."

"Do you have a few minutes?" Stephanie asked.

"Sure. Have a seat."

Stephanie closed the door, waited to see if David would object and when he didn't she crossed the room and sat down.

"Whatsup?"

"I just want to thank you for working with me this morning and for giving me this chance."

David leaned back in his chair. "I'm all about winning, Stephanie, for the team. If putting you out there as lead will do that for us, then so be it. But—" he held up his index finger "—like I said, there is no guarantee. If Kelly is ready and back in time..." He let his words trail off.

Stephanie bit down on her tongue to keep from saying what was really on her mind. She knew her words would do her more harm than good. "I understand." She tugged down on her V-neck T-shirt, showcasing a bit more cleavage and smiled inwardly when David's eyes were automatically drawn there.

"Same time tomorrow?" she asked sweetly.

David blinked. "Yes. Same time."

Slowly she stood up. "I'll be here."

David nodded as she walked out. He shook his head to clear it. Maybe spending too much alone time with Stephanie wasn't such a great idea. She oozed sex appeal and it was not lost on him. It took all his self-control not to see exactly what her treasures were beneath her skimpy track clothing. Man, he couldn't find a new assistant coach fast enough. He went back to reviewing the potential candidates, jotted down some notes and made appointments to see them within the next two days.

He glanced up at the clock on the wall above the door. Three o'clock. He'd been up since five. He rubbed his eyes and craned his stiff neck. It was definitely time to call it a day. The team was gone and the cleaning crew had also come and left.

He pushed up from his desk, stretched and arched his back. Picking up his cap from the desk he dropped it haphazardly on his head, turned out the lights and locked the doors. Today was a day for a good hot bath, stiff drink and nothing more taxing than watching television until he fell asleep.

He walked down the corridor that led to the locker and exercise rooms, just to do a last check before leaving when he heard a locker door close.

He frowned. The training camp had been burglarized on more than one occasion and his pleas for extra security had netted him nothing. Then there was always the relentless reporter who in the pursuit of a story would stoop to digging around in the locker rooms to see what dirt they could unearth.

David eased down the hall toward the sound of the noise. He pulled out his cell phone and pressed 911, ready to hit Send the instant he saw anything out of order.

He turned the corner. If it was that bastard Miller again he was…

Stephanie stood in front of him, totally naked and soaking wet. Her breasts were full and firm, her nipples were hard and alert, her stomach flat and tight. Dark pubic hair glistened from the water. She made no effort to cover herself and David couldn't seem to move. She was exquisite.

"I decided to take a shower before I left." She reached

for the towel that was on the bench but did nothing more with it than hold it in her hand. "I hope that's not a problem. I didn't know anyone else was still around."

"No problem." He still didn't move, didn't look away.

She started walking toward him. "I always have a problem getting to all the spots on my back." She handed him the towel. "Would you mind?" She turned around.

David gritted his teeth. This was not good. He needed to run, not walk to the nearest exit. But he didn't. How long had it been since he'd been with a woman? Months? His heart raced and his penis hardened. He took the towel and began to dry her back, like the fool he knew he was. He ran the towel over the column of her spine, across her hips and round rear end. As he bent to dry her thighs she turned to face him. His lips were inches away from her navel. She smelled like springtime.

She took his face in her hands and looked down into his eyes.

"I want it just as badly as you do," she said, her voice a husky whisper.

Slowly he stood. He dropped the towel.

Their first kiss was anything but tentative. It was filled with fierce urgency, raw desire and a fevered hunger. David's hands were all over Stephanie and she urged him on with moans and undulations all the while undressing him until he was stripped down to his socks.

For an instant they faced each other, stock still, their breaths coming fast and furious knowing that this was the last exit before the bridge of no return.

Stephanie stepped around to the end row of the lockers and leaned back against the smooth, cool surface. She crooked a finger, beckoning him.

David walked over, roughly clasped her hips in his hands and lifted her up. She wrapped her legs around his waist and sighed with pleasure when she felt him fill her.

Oh yes, she thought as he pushed and pulled inside her, murmuring dirty little turn-ons in her ear, everything she ever wanted was hers.

"Yeah, baby," she whispered.

When it was over they sank to the cool concrete floor. David couldn't look at Stephanie without seeing his future irrevocably changed. Finally he pulled himself together and got up to get dressed.

"There's more where that came from," Stephanie cooed, reaching up to stroke his thigh.

He looked down on her barely able to contain his disgust with her and himself. "Get dressed, Stephanie. I need to lock up."

"So it's like that, huh?"

He tightened the string on his sweatpants. "Like what?"

"Take what you want and then ignore me." She stood, hands on her hips. "Are you also going to add 'this should have never happened'?" She chuckled a nasty laugh. "Well, Dave, it did. I liked it and I know you did, too." She put on her bra and fastened it then stepped into her matching mint green panties. "But, I'm a big girl so don't worry I'm not going to stalk you or cry rape." He flinched. "Just think of it as a thank you for letting me start." She put on her T-shirt.

He stared at her, unsure how serious she was. He nodded and pulled his shirt over his head. "Fine."

She put on her shorts and sneakers. "Ready?" she asked.

He didn't respond but headed for the exit with Stephanie behind him.

Once they were outside in the parking lot he turned to her. "Listen, what happened back there, stays back there. You have your spot. Okay?"

She smiled sweetly. "Understood, coach. See you in the morning?"

"Yeah." He turned and walked to his car. What went down between them could never get out. If it did he would be ruined. He got in his car and sat there for a few minutes thinking about his options. He didn't have any. Stephanie had to be kept quiet, whatever it took.

Chapter 26

Alex tried to stay focused on his patient as he went over the rehab regime, but thoughts of Kelly and what he believed he'd discovered kept playing games with his head. First and foremost, he'd broken his own rule by becoming involved with a patient. It was stupid and he knew it, but the part of him that was all male didn't give a damn what the doctor's rule of etiquette was.

Kelly Maxwell appealed to him in a way that a woman had not in a very long time, and he knew that spelled nothing but trouble. But what could he do now? He'd already crossed the line. Not only had he sat in her company outside of the hospital, he'd actually asked her out on a date.

He had two choices: one, he could cancel the date and cancel plans to take her home after her sessions; or two, he could keep the date, keep taking her home after her sessions and stop being her doctor. Neither option was appealing but not being able to at least pursue a relationship with her was the least attractive of the two.

If he turned her over to another doctor, David would have a fit and possibly take her back to Atlanta—and then what? But if he didn't, he'd be breaking every ethic code on the books.

Finally his session was over and for the life of him he couldn't recall what he'd told the poor man. Thankfully that was his last patient of the day and he was going home.

Fortunately traffic wasn't too bad and he pulled up in front of his building in short order, parked the car and went inside. He tossed his jacket on the couch and went straight to the fridge. An icy cold beer greeted him. Screwing off the top he took a long, refreshing swallow.

Alex walked into his living room and plopped down on the couch. He reached for the remote on the end table and pointed it at the television. At least now he had an idea how David maintained such a tight hold on her, he mused as he flipped through the channels. David was her eyes and her translator. She depended on him to get through her days. But at what cost? And why wouldn't he want to see her do something about her problem?

Maybe he was jumping to conclusions. She could have had that brochure for any number of reasons. Yet he doubted it. From the little he'd observed about David, he was a control freak and her disability was the perfect way to control her. To compound her problems he was sure she had an eating disorder. All the test results pointed to it. It was the only explanation for the lack of density in her bones at her age. He wondered if David knew about that as well.

First things first, he concluded, finishing off his beer. He'd get her assigned to another doctor and he would only consult. David would just have to be pissed off. He'd talk to Dr. Logan in the morning and see if he had room in his schedule to work with Kelly. Hopefully having the chief of staff work with Kelly would appease David enough to let her stay in New York and finish her treatment. Then he'd work on getting Kelly out of David's grip. Maybe then they'd have a chance at something—if she wanted it. His gut told him that she did.

The following morning, Alex was waiting for Bert Logan when he arrived at his office.

"To what do I owe a visit from you?" Bert asked with a smile.

"Need to talk to you about something."

"Sure, come on in." He unlocked his office door and let them in. "Coffee?"

"No. Thanks. I've already had my fill."

Bert looked at him curiously. "That serious, huh? Must be a woman." He put the coffee on then sat down. He folded his hands on his desk. "I'm listening."

"I need to be taken off of a case and I want you to handle it."

Bert leaned back. The corner of his mouth quirked upward in a half grin. "Who is she?"

"Kelly Maxwell."

"The track star?"

"One and the same."

Bert twisted his lips in thought, a slow frown brewing across his forehead. "You want to tell me what's going on?"

Alex braced his arms on his thighs and blew out a breath. He looked up at Bert hoping that their years of friendship would stand up to this test and not allow hospital politics to interfere.

Slowly he began and laid it all out on the table. When he'd finished silence hung between them and he was sure that Bert was going to explode.

Bert suddenly pushed up from his desk and stood. He ran his right hand through his shock of gray hair. He turned toward Alex with a look of utter bafflement on his face. His blue eyes darkened.

"Damn, man don't you ever do anything easy? Do you totally want to screw up your career?" He began to pace. "Does anyone on staff know that you've been to her place?"

"No."

"I don't want this hospital to be sued. And from what you've told me about this Livingston guy, it's just the thing he would do." He pointed his finger at Alex. "And you my friend would be ground beef." He shoved his hands into the pockets of his lab coat. "Bring me her case file. I'll take a look." He paused then looked Alex dead in the eye. "Have you slept with her?"

"No."

"Thank God for small favors." He blew out a relieved breath. "Lucky for you you're so damned good at what you do or I'd have your ass up on charges. Friend or no friend."

"Duly noted." He stood. "I'll have Ruby bring down her file this afternoon."

"When is Ms. Maxwell due back?"

"Tomorrow."

"Gee that gives me plenty of time to rearrange my life," he said, sarcastically.

"Look, I appreciate this Bert."

"I know you do. And you owe me. A golf game."

Alex groaned. Bert knew how much he hated golf. "Sure, name the day and time and I'll be there."

"I'll let you know. And be sure to bring your smile with you. Now get on outta here before I change my mind."

Alex chuckled lightly in relief. "Thanks again." He walked out and shut the door behind him.

Now for the hard part, he thought, getting Kelly to trust him enough to tell him what was really going on with her so that they could work on it together. And while they worked on her problems they could work on a relationship.

He went to his office and closed the door. For several minutes he stared at the phone, debating. Finally, he picked up the phone and dialed.

Chapter 27

Kelly was stretched out on the couch going over the information that Ms. Stevens had given her when the phone rang. As she reached for the phone, she hoped it wasn't David again.

"Hello?"

"Kelly. It's Dr. Hutchinson."

Her expression immediately brightened. She sat up straighter and put the booklets aside. "Hi. Is…anything wrong?"

"No. Actually I was wondering if maybe we could meet somewhere…to talk. Maybe the restaurant in the hotel so you won't have to travel."

"O-kay," she said a bit hesitant. "Are you sure everything is all right?"

Yes, fine." Of course it really wasn't. "I can be there in about an hour."

"I'll meet you in the lobby."

"Great. See you soon."

Kelly hung up with a mixture of confusion and excitement. It was great that Alex wanted to see her, but the question was why.

Well, if she was going to meet him in the restaurant, she certainly needed something on more flattering than her pajamas. She got up from the couch and walked, limped to her bedroom to find something appropriate to put on. She pulled open her closet and went into panic mode. Her entire wardrobe consisted of sweatpants, T-shirts and oversize sweaters. Not that she had a lot of going out outfits to choose from but the few she did have she hadn't brought from Atlanta.

She chewed on the tip of her finger, thinking. Then she remembered she'd stuck an ankle-length Indian gauze skirt in her suitcase and she'd put it in her dresser drawer instead of hanging it up. She went to the drawer, took it out and held it in front of her. Perfect. She could wear the pale green and yellow skirt with a yellow tank top.

Kelly checked the bedside clock. He said an hour. She'd already spent fifteen of those precious minutes looking for something to wear and she still needed time to get ready. She sat down on the side of the bed and gingerly took off her space boot then unwrapped her ankle. Gently she massaged her calf and then her ankle, then her foot. She reached for her crutches, stood up and headed for the bathroom. She couldn't risk falling in the shower so she'd take a quick bath. She'd gotten that down to an art.

Twenty minutes later she was in front of the mirror pulling her hair into a ponytail and checking the pimple that was beginning to erupt on her chin. Not much she could do about it now other than wish it away. She blotted the shine off her nose with a tissue and added lip gloss to her mouth. That was the extent of her makeup.

She stepped back and took a look at her reflection. Why couldn't she be beautiful? Why couldn't she have flawless skin? Why couldn't she feel better about who she was? She turned away from the questions. Well, at least for a little while she could pretend to be all the things she knew she wasn't.

She picked up her purse from the end of the bed, tucked her crutches beneath her arms and walked out.

The hotel lobby was moderately busy with a steady flow of guests and hotel staff. She stood near the registration desk and spotted Alex the moment he walked in.

He was casually dressed in a pair of faded blue jeans and a pale blue long-sleeved Oxford shirt, open at the neck. Kelly waved to get his attention.

"Hi. Sorry if I kept you waiting. Traffic was a mess for some reason."

"Not a problem. I just came down."

"Well let's go in and get a table so you can get off your feet. How are you feeling by the way?" he asked, placing his hand on her lower back as they walked toward the hotel restaurant.

"Pretty good actually."

He nodded.

"Two for dinner?" the hostess asked when they entered.

"Yes," Alex said.

"Right this way." She showed them to their table and placed down the menus. "Would you like something to drink while you look over the menu?"

"I'll have iced tea," Kelly said.

"Same here."

"Coming right up."

"So..." Kelly hesitated. "Why did you need to see me?"

Alex chuckled a bit nervously. "You don't beat around the bush do you?"

She shrugged. "Not if I really want to know something."

Alex glanced off for a second then looked back at her. "Okay, I'll get straight to the point. But hear me out first."

"All right."

"I'm giving your case to another doctor." He held up his hand when he saw she was about to protest. "He's the chief of staff. The best. I trained under him."

"I don't understand. Why?"

He took a breath. "I think it's the best thing to do...because if not, my continuing to treat you would go against ethics and hospital policy."

She frowned in confusion. "What are you talking about? When we came to New York it was because you agreed to be my doctor. Is there something wrong, something you aren't telling me?"

"I want you to be seen by another doctor because—"

"Because what? You have more important clients? You're too busy? You don't think my case is worthy of your precious time—"

"No. Because I want to see you...outside of the hospital, not as a patient."

Kelly stopped cold. "What?" she stammered, needing to be sure she heard him correctly.

"I want to see you Kelly. I want to take you out, get to know you. If you want to. And if you don't I can understand that, too, and I'll back off if you say so."

She didn't know what to say. It was what she'd secretly hoped but never imagined would really happen. "I..."

"It's okay. It was stupid of me to be so presumptuous."

The waitress arrived with their drinks. "Are you ready to order or do you need some more time?" She looked from one to the other.

"Give us a few more minutes," Alex said.

Kelly toyed with her napkin until the waitress was gone. "What do we tell David?" she finally said and a smile of delight spread across Alex's face. She grinned.

"I'll handle David."

"Good luck." She looked at him. "I live in Atlanta," she said slowly as the reality of the direction they were heading in began to settle with her. "And you live here." Her comment hung in the air for a moment.

"I know. I like Atlanta and you could get to like New York. We'll take it one day at a time and see how it goes. No commitments, no pressure or unreasonable expectations. Let's get to know each other."

"Are you sure?"

"As sure as I can be. I know that if I continue to treat you I would lose my objectivity and I can't risk that happening. You getting better is a primary objective, bar none." He never wanted to be the one to tell her any bad news, not like what happened with Leigh. He'd made the mistake once of falling for a patient and continuing to be their doctor. It wouldn't happen again.

"One day at a time," she repeated.

He nodded.

She folded her hands atop the table. "So...since you're no longer officially my doctor, is this our first official date?"

His dark eyes caught the light and sparkled. "Yeah, I guess it is."

She smiled sweetly. "In that case, I'll have the lobster bisque to start."

Alex tossed his head back and laughed from deep in his gut. "Anything the lady wants."

They ordered their meal and talked in generalities as they ate. Alex told her all about Dr. Logan and his credentials and assured her that she was in the best of hands with him.

Alex listened to her tell him about life in the fast lane of track and field, some of the characters on the team and the places that she'd been. Minute by minute he was becoming more enamored of her. She was funny, intelligent, warm spirited and to him a beautiful woman. She presented herself as strong and independent but he knew better. Beneath the outer shell was a woman who had a laundry list of self-doubt. He wanted to change that. He wanted to be there when she bloomed into all the woman that she could be.

Suddenly she stopped speaking. "Why are you staring at me like that? Do I have salad in my teeth?"

Her question ended his reverie. "No. I was just thinking how pretty you are, how much I'm enjoying being with you."

She lowered her gaze. "I'm not pretty."

He reached across the table and took her hand. "Why would you say that?" he asked, frowning.

"Because it's true. Look at me. I'm a basket of features. A little of this, a little of that. Nothing matches. Apples and oranges."

"But don't you know that's what makes you so absolutely appealing? You have a unique beauty that is magnified by who you are inside. You have incredible eyes, a wonderful mouth, sweeping brows and silky lashes. And that cleft in your chin is pretty cute, too."

She almost smiled.

"Look at me." When she did he continued. "I think you're beautiful. But it doesn't really matter what I think, it's what you think. Stop comparing yourself to what the magazines say are beautiful. Look in the mirror and tell it to yourself."

"Easier said than done."

"Maybe but you should give it a shot." He cut into his steak.

"Can I be honest with you about something?"

Alex looked up. "Sure."

"I was kinda hoping that…you wanted something more…"

He put down his knife and fork. "You did?'

She smiled. "Yes."

"And why is that?"

"Because I did, too."

"I'm glad. I was really reluctant about laying my cards on the table. I wasn't sure how you would take it or if you were even interested. Not sure what I would have done if you'd told me to get lost."

"Has a woman ever said that to you?"

"Not yet." He grinned. "But there's a first time for everything."

"Excuse me." They both looked up at the waitress. "Will you be having dessert or coffee?"

"Do you want dessert?" Alex asked.

"No. Thanks. I'm fine." She knew she'd have to get rid of what she'd ingested already.

"We're good. Can you bring me the check?"

"Sure. I'll be right back."

Alex waited a beat, debating whether or not this was the right time to divulge what he suspected. But he didn't want them getting off on the wrong foot with secrets and lies.

"Listen, there's something I think I should tell you before we go any further." He looked into her inquiring eyes. "When I was at your place the other day and I went to get my jacket, I, uh, came across some brochures in one of the jacket pockets."

Kelly drew in a sharp breath.

"They were about dyslexia."

She glanced around the room avoiding eye contact with him. "They aren't mine."

"Kelly, if they are, and I say if, it's okay. It would explain so much."

"Well there's nothing to explain because I already told you they're not mine!" She was beginning to panic and her stomach rolled.

"It's nothing to be ashamed of—"

She pushed up from the table and grabbed her crutches from the empty chair. "You don't know what you're talking about. I'm tired. Thanks for dinner. I'm going up to my room."

Alex stood and held her arm. "Don't run away."

"I'm not running." She held her head down, unable to look at him.

"Is that the hold that David has over you?"

Her head snapped up.

"How long has he known?" he asked gently.

The stiffness of her body began to soften. Slowly she sat back down as if suddenly deflated.

"I've always been so ashamed," she murmured. She pressed her fist to her mouth.

"There's no reason to be ashamed, Kelly. None. Everyone has something that they have to deal with." He thought about his own bouts with alcohol and the guilt he still carried in his heart about Leigh.

She looked across the table and into his eyes. "Do you have any idea what it feels like to be ridiculed, to always feel like an idiot, to know that something was wrong but not know what it was?" She breathed hard and fast. "It's been like that all my life. I was the butt of jokes in school, teased by the kids, ridiculed by the teachers." Her eyes filled with tears. She snatched up a napkin from the table and wiped her eyes then sighed deeply, the old wounds reopening.

"It was all a vicious cycle." She looked off into the distance. "I'd be made fun of in school so I stayed by myself pretty much. So for company I would eat. By ten I'd really begun to put on weight. I wasn't just dumb anymore, I was fat, too." She laughed derisively. "More ammunition for my tormentors. That's when they began beating me up after school. I'd have to run home every day." Her voice cracked. "But you can't run very fast if you're fat. So I started throwing up my food after I ate to lose weight. Then I'd eat because I was lonely, get chased home because I was dumb and fat and the cycle just continued."

Alex listened in rapt silence. His gut twisted. He couldn't imagine what she must have gone through, how she'd felt. But kids can be so very cruel. What was worst in his mind, however, were the adults in her life that let her fall through the cracks.

"As I started getting taller I began to thin out a little bit and the running actually helped to keep the weight down. Back then, especially in Mississippi where I grew up, no one really cared if little black kids could read or write, so they kept passing me from grade to grade. The only way I kept my sanity was by joining the track team in high school. That's when I met David."

She told him about how David discovered her disability and promised to always take care of her. Alex wished he could choke David for what he'd done to Kelly.

Kelly looked at him. "Still want to date me?" she asked with a crooked smile filled with humiliation.

"What you told me changes nothing. If anything I'm even more drawn to you. Regardless of what you may think, it takes strength and ingenuity to go through what you've done and still have a life, a good one at that. At least to some degree. And what's more important is that you've finally taken the steps to change. That takes courage."

"You make it all sound so noble." She sighed and shook her head. "I've dreaded anyone ever finding out—the public, the media, the team." She gave a little shiver.

"Listen to me." He held her hands, his voice filled with urgency. "Millions of people suffer with dyslexia: actors, models, businessmen and women. You're not alone." He paused. "And if you let me, I'll be right there for you."

"Do you really mean that?"

"Yeah, I really do."

"I don't know what to say."

"Why don't you start with telling me what you've found out so far?"

She pressed her lips together. "Well..."

Kelly told him all about her visit to the clinic and the tests and classes and what Ms. Stevens told her.

"That's great. How do you feel about it?"

"Excited. Hopeful." She smiled, her eyes lighting up.

The waitress returned with the check.

Alex reached in his back pants pocket, took out his wallet and credit card and handed the card to the waitress. "Thanks," he said.

"There's one other thing we haven't discussed," he said to Kelly.

"What?"

"Your eating problem."

She looked away.

"That can be dealt with, too. And I'm pretty sure it's the reason why you sustained the kind of injury that you did. But you're going to need counseling, ongoing to beat it."

She didn't respond.

"It's dangerous, Kelly and life threatening. You do understand that don't you?"

Reluctantly she nodded.

"I'm sure I can find a doctor that would be willing to work with you."

She looked dead at him. "Why are you doing all this? What's in it for you?"

"Is that what you think, that I'm personally going to benefit somehow?"

"That's the way it's always been. No one has ever done anything for me if there was nothing in it for them."

"I'm not David."

She flinched then lowered her gaze. "I know," she breathed. "I'm sorry."

"Kelly, sometimes people do things for others simply because they care about the person and want the best for them. No more, no less."

The waitress returned with his card and the check.

He took both, signed the receipt and gave it back. "Come on, I'll take you back to your room."

* * *

They stood in front of her door.

"Thanks for dinner," she said, looking up at him.

"Thank you for trusting me."

They faced each other for an awkward moment.

"I guess I better get going," he finally said. "Have a full day tomorrow."

Kelly nodded. "Will I see you at the clinic?"

"I'll be sure to stop in and check on you." He paused a beat. "Good night."

"Good night."

He started to leave.

"Hutch…"

He turned. "Yes?"

"Do you have any rules of ethics about a kiss on a first date?"

A slow smile inched across his mouth as he stepped up to her. "As a matter of fact—" he tilted her chin up with the tip of his finger "—I ripped that page right out of the book." He lowered his head and tenderly touched his lips to hers in a slow exploration.

Kelly's mouth parted ever so slightly when his arm went around her waist, holding her securely against him. She sighed into his mouth and let her body relax against his.

He pressed a bit harder, slipping his tongue into her mouth to play with hers. He groaned deep in his throat and Kelly felt suddenly light-headed, thankful that he held her so tight. She felt his growing erection press between her thighs even as she grew damp with desire.

Slowly he released her and her eyes fluttered open, the dream ending. He was breathing hard, his dark complexion flushed. He swallowed then ran his tongue across his lips.

"I really think I need to get out of here before we get into something we may not be ready for."

Her smile was coy and full of promise. "Whenever you are," she murmured, turned and walked inside, shutting the door behind her.

Alex pressed the button for the elevator and quickly stepped inside before he took her up on her obvious offer. But on the way down, her question plagued him. Why was he really doing this? Was it because he really cared or because he wanted to somehow make atonement for what had happened with Leigh? *No one does something for no reason.* His taunt to David returned to haunt him.

Chapter 28

"Glad we talked," David was saying to Herb Townes the prospective assistant coach. "Your experience and credentials are impressive."

Herb nodded. "Track and field is in my blood." He chuckled. "My father was a coach and so was my grandfather. I know I can bring a lot to the team and take some of the pressure off you."

David smiled. "I could certainly use some of that." He was thoughtful for a moment. "Why don't we go out on the track and you can get a look at the team in action."

"Sounds great."

They went out onto the field where the women were preparing for the 200 meters.

"Is that Stephanie Daniels in the green?" Herb asked.

"Yes." He pulled his cap onto his head.

"She's got skills. I've been watching her for a while, but she's always been overshadowed by Kelly Maxwell."

"Well, Kelly is the superstar. She's won more medals for this team than the whole team combined."

"Will she be in shape for the preliminaries?"

"That's the plan."

The women took off from the starting blocks and David and Herb zeroed in on them as they sped around the track.

"Wow," Herb said in awe as he watched Stephanie.

David checked the watch. She was going for a record. His heart started to race. Stephanie made the turn passing one then another of the leaders until they were afterthoughts. She crossed the finish line in front of the others with plenty of room to spare.

Herb turned to David. "If she can run like that you may not have to worry whether Kelly gets back in time."

David didn't comment but he was thinking the very same thing. "Come and let me introduce you to the team."

Once everyone was gathered around near the clubhouse, David made his announcement.

"As you all know, Reggie is still in the hospital and...we're not sure when he is going to be well enough to come back. That being the case, I've had no other choice than to start looking for a new assistant coach to fill Reggie's spot during his absence." He turned to Herb. "I'd like you all to meet and welcome your new assistant coach, Herb Townes."

Herb was just as surprised by the impromptu announcement as the team. For a moment he was at a loss but quickly pulled himself together.

"I know what it's like to have a coach that you have established a close relationship with over the years," he began. "And I'm sure that each of you have a special relationship with Reggie. So trust me on this, I have no intention of trying to fill his shoes because I know that I can't. But what I can do is give you my absolute best and work like hell to get the best out of each of you. I know that Coach Livingston and I have the same goal in mind, a winning team. And if we all work together, I know we can do it." He looked from one expectant face to the next. "I've been watching your tapes and keeping up with your stats for a while, but videos and numbers can't replace knowing the individual. I'm looking forward to getting to know each of you."

David slapped him a couple of times on the back then shook his hand. "Welcome aboard."

"Thanks, David," he said so that only David could hear him. "I won't let you down."

David nodded, then looked out at the team. "Okay everybody enough fun and games, back to work. You still have another hour." He walked with Herb back to the office.

"You don't waste time, do you?" Herb asked.

"When I know something is right, I go after it. I feel you're the man for the job. No sense in dragging the process out." He sat down behind his desk, opened the file drawer and withdrew some papers. He looked them over then handed them to Herb. "I'll need you to fill these out."

Herb pulled the paperwork toward him and began filling out the forms.

Now that David had a capable person to run the day to day activities with the team, he could concentrate on Kelly and hopefully get Stephanie out of his hair before things got too far out of hand. He'd give Herb a week or two to get acclimated to the team then he would head back out to

New York. The idea of Kelly spending too much unsupervised time with Hutchinson rubbed him in all the wrong ways.

Herb finished up with the forms and gave them back to David who looked them over.

"Everything seems to be in order." He stuck the files in a folder on his desk. "You can start first thing tomorrow. Nine o'clock."

Herb stood and stuck out his hand. "I'll be here and thanks again."

David shook his hand. "I think this will be a great partnership."

"So do I." He turned and walked out.

Several moments later there was a knock on his office door.

"Come in."

It was Stephanie. David kept his expression emotionless.

"What can I do for you?"

Stephanie gave him a coy smile as she closed and locked the door behind her. "I think you already gave me what I wanted yesterday." She crossed the room and sat down opposite him.

"That was yesterday. It's over and done."

"Really?"

"Yes, really."

"Now David," she cooed, "that's no way to be. We had such a good time yesterday and I know you enjoyed it as much as I did."

"Stephanie, it was a mistake."

She got up and came around to his side of the desk and knelt down in front of it. "I don't make mistakes," she said as she unzipped his pants.

He grabbed her hands. "Get up, Stephanie."

"I only want to show you my appreciation." She pulled

her hands out of his grip and reached inside his pants. He drew in a sharp breath. "Sit back, relax and enjoy," she whispered before taking him into her mouth.

David leaned back and squeezed his eyes shut as the exquisite pleasure raced through him. This couldn't continue he thought even as his body betrayed him. He'd have to find a way to nip this in the bud and quickly. He held her head in the palms of his hands. But in the meantime he may as well enjoy what she was willing to give.

"You turned the case over to Dr. Logan?" Ruby asked incredulously. "Why? I think I already know the answer but I want to hear it come out of your mouth." Her lips twisted in annoyance.

"No lectures, okay?"

"We'll see." She put her hands on hips as she stood over his desk.

"I made the mistake once of getting involved with a patient. I don't want to make that mistake again."

"So you think that by handing her off to Dr. Logan that somehow absolves you of any wrongdoing?"

"Yes. Technically she's no longer my patient."

Ruby sighed and shook her head. "And I'm the Easter Bunny. Hutch, what is wrong with you?"

He looked away from her accusing eyes. "I want to get to know her and I know I can't do that if she's my patient. I know it sounds crazy to you and maybe it is, but...I really care about her and I want to be able to freely see where it can go."

Ruby finally sat down. "Hutch, she lives in Atlanta. You live here in New York. What do you think is going to happen when her treatment is over? She's going to go back home," she said, answering her own question. "Then what?

Are you going to follow her all over the world as she goes from one tournament to the next—if she can ever run again? Have you thought about that?"

"Yeah, I have."

"And?"

"We'll deal with it when it comes to that. But I'll never know if I don't give it a shot." He took a breath and looked Ruby in her eyes. "I haven't felt this strongly about anyone since Leigh."

"Is that what this is really all about, a cleansing of your conscience?"

"I don't know. All I do know is that I want to try."

"Hutch, have you given any thought to what it will do to her if you suddenly wake up one day and realize that the only reason you got involved with her was because you wanted to do for her what you couldn't do for Leigh?"

"Leigh may be part of it. I'll admit that. But not in the way that you think. Last night I went over everything in my head about me and Leigh; what went wrong and what went right. I made promises to her that were impossible to keep. It destroyed her and nearly destroyed me. I'm not going to do that again. And the only way I cannot fall into that trap is to stay away from Kelly as her doctor."

"But you are a doctor. Do you think for one minute that she is not going to ask you what you think, what her prognosis is, no matter what Dr. Logan tells her? If you allow yourself to truly fall for this girl, do you think you won't try to do everything in your power to get her back to the athlete she once was? If you don't think you will then you're a fool. And you may be a lot of things, Hutch, but you are not a fool." Slowly she stood. "You know I want you to be happy, right?"

"Yes."

She blew out a breath. "Then be happy." A shadow of a smile eased the tight lines around her eyes. "And be honest with her, no matter what."

He glanced up at her. "I intend to."

She reached toward his desk and snatched Kelly's file then tucked it under her arm. "You won't be needing this." She arched a challenging brow when he started to protest. "And don't you even think about setting foot in the rehab room when she's here," she warned, wagging a finger at him. "I mean it." With that she spun away and marched toward the door. She stopped with her hand on the knob and glanced at him over her shoulder. "Have a nice day."

Alex chuckled as she shut the door behind her. He checked his watch. He had surgery in an hour. Hopefully, barring any complications, he should be finished with the knee replacement in two hours. By that time Kelly should be finished with her therapy and they could spend the rest of the day together.

Chapter 29

Alex was waiting at the exit door as Kelly came out of rehab.

"Hi," she said, a shy smile on her face.

"Hi, yourself. How'd it go today?"

"Pretty good. Dr. Logan is nice and he had good things to say about you."

"That's encouraging." He grinned and held the door open for her. "I was thinking that I could drop you off at the hotel."

"I'd like that, but I need to go to my class. They start today."

"Oh, okay. Well…"

"I could use a lift." She smiled.

"And a lift you shall have. Right this way, ma'am."

Once inside the car she gave him the address for the center.

"I'm really curious to see how this whole meditation thing works," she said while she fastened her seatbelt.

"It's all the rage," he said in a bad imitation of a bourgeois lilt.

Kelly giggled.

"How's the ankle feeling?"

"Better. I worked without the brace today and it felt pretty good. Dr. Logan seemed pleased."

Alex nodded. "Did he take any X-rays or a new MRI?" he asked, the doctor in him taking over.

"No. Not today."

"Hmm." He should have especially after her first session without the brace. He'd have to speak with Bert. But then Ruby's warning voice began shouting in his head. She was right. It was going to be hard to not play doctor when that's what he was.

"Do you think he should have? Was it wrong for him not to?" Her voice held a note of alarm.

He shot her a glance. "Dr. Logan is the best. He knows what he's doing. If he believed there was no reason for an X-ray or MRI then there wasn't one."

"What would you have done?"

He wanted to tell her he would have ordered the test, but he didn't. "The same thing Dr. Logan did." He stopped for a light. "Are you busy later this evening?"

"No."

"Would you like to see a movie?"

"Okay."

"Great. I'll pick you up around seven. Is that good?"

"That's fine."

"How long is this class?"

"Ms. Stevens said an hour. So I should be finished by four."

"I'll come back and get you if you want. Or I can just wait."

"I couldn't ask you to do that."

"You didn't. I offered."

"You really don't have to...but since you insist." She grinned. "Sure, come back and pick me up. I'd appreciate it."

"Not a problem." He pulled to a stop in front of the building, got out and came around to her side and opened the door. "Will you be all right from here?" He helped her out of the car.

"I'll be fine. Thanks." She looked up at him. "Are you sure you really want to do this?"

"Do what, pick you up after class?" he asked, full of feigned innocence.

"No, set out on a relationship with me."

"Yes, I'm sure. Are you?"

"Yeah."

"Well, there you have it folks. The votes are in. They're gonna go for the gold." He chuckled, leaned down and lightly kissed her forehead. "Have a good class. I'll see you in an hour."

"Okay."

He watched her go inside before pulling off. Yes, he was very sure.

Kelly stood waiting in front of the elevator to go up to the second floor where the classes were being held when her cell phone rang. She glanced down at the number. David.

She removed the phone from the clip on her side. "Hello."

"Hey, Kelly. It's David."

"Hi. How are you?"

"The question is, how are you?"

"I'm fine."

"It sounds noisy. Where are you, still at the hospital?"

"Uh, yes."

"Is the ambulette coming to pick you up?"

"Yes. I'm uh, waiting for it now."

"Good. Well, I was calling with some good news."

"Reggie's better?"

"No unfortunately, he's still the same. But I just hired a new assistant coach."

"That's great."

"He starts tomorrow. And once I get him acclimated to the routine I can get back up there to New York."

Her stomach tightened. "Oh...wonderful. But there's no need to rush on my account. I'm fine."

"I want to see that for myself. So hopefully I'll be back in about two weeks."

The elevator doors opened.

"Hello? Are you still there?"

"Yes, I'm here," she murmured, stepping aside as several people got off.

"Did you hear what I said? I'll be back in two weeks."

"Yeah, that's...good news." She got on the elevator. "Well, I have to go."

"The ambulette is there?"

"Yes," she lied.

"All right. I'll give you a call later on this evening."

"Sure. Thanks for calling."

She didn't have to bother to hang up. When the doors closed she was thankfully disconnected.

Two weeks, she thought as the elevator rose. Two weeks and her life would revert to the way it was. She couldn't let that happen.

* * *

David held the phone in his hand. He didn't like how Kelly sounded on the phone. The sooner he got back to New York the better. And the quicker she got better and back in Atlanta where she belonged the quicker things could get back to normal. He stared sightlessly at the opposite wall. Maybe there was a way he could speed up the process.

He picked up the phone and dialed.

Chapter 30

"You did what?" Charisse asked, stunned by her cousin's confession. But then again she shouldn't be. Stephanie always had a wild streak.

"I did it right there in the locker room." Stephanie laughed. She didn't tell her about the office escapade. That would be a bit much for her conservative cousin.

"Steph, why would you do something like that? It can only lead to trouble."

"I know what I'm doing, cuz. Once I have David wrapped around my little sexy finger, Kelly Maxwell won't stand a chance. And if I have to resort to using what happened between us as leverage, I'll do it."

"Steph, listen, don't even go down that road. It's not worth it."

"Not worth it! Are you kidding me? Do you know what I would be worth financially if I get a shot at the title? I'd have endorsements coming out my behind. I could write my own ticket. I'd be set, Charisse. Do you understand? I'd be set. And I'll be damned if I'm gonna let some overrated has-been take what should be mine."

"Everyone gets what they deserve in this life. You'll get what's coming to you in due time. You don't have to manipulate people to get it. It will eventually catch up with you."

"Have you found religion or something? You sound like one of the church mothers from back home." She stretched out on her couch and put her feet up. "Or maybe it's the fact that you are with child that has you talking all sanctimonious."

Charisse cringed when her own dilemma was tossed into the forefront.

Stephanie's tough talk softened. "Have you told him yet?"

"No."

"What are you waiting for?"

"I'm still deciding what I'm going to do."

"Well if you don't decide something soon the decision will be taken out of your hands."

"I know."

"Why don't you go to his job and tell him. He's sure not to make a scene at his place of business. Didn't you say he was some kind of doctor?"

"Yes. Rehab specialist."

Stephanie frowned for a moment, the kernel of a thought trying to form but she couldn't pull it together. "Like I said, go to his place of employment."

"I couldn't do that."

Stephanie sighed heavily. "Fine. You know what's best for you. Just don't wait too long or you'll wind up stuck all the way around. Who knows, he might even be happy about it."

"That would be ideal but highly unlikely."

"Let me ask you this, and be honest. What do you really want?"

"If I had a choice I'd want the whole package, the husband, the house, the kids." She chuckled sadly. "Idealistic."

"Not if it's what you want. I don't have those kinds of aspirations, but you do. That's what's important. Anyway, I gotta run. Early day tomorrow. Dave has me coming in at six to train. So I need to be rested and refreshed, after I get back from dinner with some friends."

"Okay. Thanks for calling to check on me."

"Sure. And don't forget what I said."

"You don't forget what I said," Charisse countered.

"Later, cuz." Stephanie laughed.

"Later."

Charisse hung up the phone and leaned back against the headboard of her bed. She knew part of Stephanie's advice was right. She did need to make a decision and it was only right, no matter what she decided to do, that Alex be told. She chewed on the tips of her freshly manicured nails.

She'd tell him. Soon. She was running out of time, but maybe his reaction to her news would seal her decision.

Charisse got up, deciding to change clothes and go for a walk. She hadn't eaten dinner and she didn't feel like fixing anything, but in a city like Manhattan there were tons of restaurants and outdoor cafes to choose from. When she got tired she'd stop somewhere for dinner. Besides, she owed herself a treat. And a nice dinner under the stars on a warm night was just the ticket.

With that in mind, she was already beginning to feel better. For tonight she would put thoughts of Alex and her current dilemma on the back burner. She'd deal with it tomorrow.

* * *

"That movie was hilarious," Kelly said as she and Alex walked out of the theater.

"Yeah, it was good. I didn't think I was going to like it. I usually go for the high action, shoot 'em up car chases."

Kelly laughed. "You seem like you would enjoy more of the intellectual movies, foreign films."

He shrugged. "Hmm, sometimes. I have to be in the mood." He steered her toward the corner with a gentle hand at the small of her back. "Hungry?"

"A little."

"That's good." He hesitated before posing his question. "Did you keep down what you ate today?"

"Yes. Today was a good day all the way around."

Alex nodded in approval. "So what do you have a taste for?"

"Pasta."

"Then pasta it is. I know a great place up on Broadway and Ninety-Sixth Street."

"Sounds good to me."

"How's the ankle?"

She smiled up at him. "Feeling pretty good, doc."

He smirked. "Sorry. Old habits die hard."

"I don't mind. Really."

"Yeah, but I don't want it to seem that I'm hovering. It's just that I am concerned. I don't want you to overdo it before it's time."

"I won't. I'm sure Dr. Logan won't let me, and I'm pretty sure you won't either."

"Have you spoken to David about the change in doctors?"

She shook her head. "No. But I will."

"How do you think he's going to take it?"

"He'll probably be upset, but he'll have to get over it that's all. I need to think about me and not worry about David's reaction. I've done that for far too long."

Alex glanced at her as they walked toward the car, seeing the look of resolve on her face. Kelly Maxwell was not only getting stronger in body but in spirit, too, and that was definitely a good thing.

David returned to his apartment from his impromptu meeting. He tossed the package on the table and stared at it for several minutes. He knew the transaction he'd just made was illegal and if he got caught he would be finished in the sports world. It was a chance he was willing to risk. Whatever it took to get Stephanie off his back he was willing to do. She was becoming a liability and he didn't see the situation getting any better anytime soon.

He took his cell phone off the clip at his waist and dialed Kelly. In just a few more weeks he'd see her and start getting things back to the way they should be.

David listened to the phone ring until her voice message came on. He frowned, disconnected the call and tried again. Voice mail. He continued to call every twenty minutes for the next two hours with no better results. Visions of Kelly and Alex played havoc with his mind. He paced his apartment like a caged tiger, tossing pillows, slamming doors and hurling expletives around the room.

He must get her back to Atlanta, and soon.

Chapter 31

"Parking is always at a premium in Manhattan," Alex said as he circled the block for the third time. "We'll have to park in the lot up the street." He drove off and put the car in the parking garage and they slowly walked back toward the restaurant. "It's right around the corner," he said.

"It's such a beautiful night out, even for New York." She laughed.

"There's definitely something about New York that draws people from all over the world. We may not have the ideal weather and rolling hills and peach trees but we certainly have everything else. It is the only city in the world that you can walk out of your house at any time of day or night and find something open, hundreds of cars on the street and the mass transit system running."

"That's true. Back home if you don't get to where you're going by ten you may as well stay home."

"Now that would drive me—"

"Alex?"

He turned at the sound of his name and stopped short. "Charisse…hi."

She got up from her table at the outdoor café, stepped around the wooden fencing and walked up to him. She looked at Kelly and gave her a tight smile then turned to Alex. "How are you?"

"Good. Having dinner?" he asked lifting his chin in the direction she'd come from.

"Yes. I didn't feel like staying in tonight." She glanced at Kelly waiting for an introduction.

"Uh, Charisse this is Kelly."

"Nice to meet you Kelly."

"You, too," Kelly replied wondering about the tension that shot sparks between Charisse and Alex. She'd never seen Alex look so utterly uncomfortable.

Charisse looked at her closer. "Kelly Maxwell, the sprinter?"

"Yes."

She glanced at Kelly's ankle then at Alex. "So you're one of Alex's patients?"

"No, actually I'm not."

Alex didn't like where this was going and was about to say his goodbyes.

"Kelly, I'm sorry, but can you excuse us for one second?"

"Sure."

Charisse took Alex's arm and steered him out of earshot.

"Charisse, not here, not now," he said before she had a chance to get started.

"No place will be a good place, but I still thought that you should know even if we aren't an item anymore."

He frowned. "Know what? What are you talking about?"

"I'm pregnant."

His expression froze even as all the air left his lungs. He swallowed. "Are you sure?"

"Very. I didn't plan this if that's what you're thinking."

He shot a glance in Kelly's direction. She was studying the menu posted on the outside of the café.

"I can't talk about this now. I'll call you tomorrow."

"Sure. My numbers are still the same."

He stared at her for a moment, unsure of what it was that he felt about her and her jarring news. "Tomorrow."

She nodded, watched him walk back to Kelly and they continued down the street and around the corner.

Charisse stood there feeling foolish, and very alone. That was a dumb, idiotic thing to do. Stop a man on the street and tell him you're carrying his child—while he's with another woman. What in the hell had gotten into her? She wasn't impulsive like that by nature. But it was just that when she saw Alex with another woman she kind of snapped and did the first thing that came to her mind—find a way to ruin his evening. That was something Stephanie would do. Wait until she told her high-strung cousin that Kelly Maxwell was not only screwing up her life but Charisse's as well.

"Are you all right?" Kelly asked as they were seated at their table. "You haven't said a word since we ran into your friend and you look like you saw a ghost."

He forced himself to smile and look into her eyes. "Hey I'm sorry. That was a former girlfriend of mine."

"I gathered as much."

"We'd been seeing each other for a while. Broke up—officially not too long ago."

"She's very pretty," Kelly said.

Alex nodded absently.

Kelly angled her head to the right. "I won't pry. But if you want to talk about it…"

Alex reached for his glass of water and took a long swallow. He'd promised himself that when he started down this road with Kelly he was going to be honest. He didn't want any secrets between them.

"She told me she's pregnant," he said as if in a dream.

Kelly's stomach instantly knotted. She blinked to get him back in focus. "Oh," was all she could figure out to say.

He sighed heavily. "I told her that I would call her tomorrow and that we would talk."

"That's, uh, a good thing," she said. "How do you feel about it?" She held her breath.

He looked straight at her. "I don't really know. Stunned, confused, angry, sad. It's not what I want for my life right now."

The waiter arrived to take their orders and Kelly was suddenly starving.

During dinner they talked about anything that had nothing to do with the elephant that had suddenly tramped into the fragile beginning of their relationship. Kelly didn't know what to feel: thankful that he was honest with her as he could have easily lied, or completely disillusioned for believing for a moment that anything could come of the two of them.

On the ride back to her hotel, they allowed the music from the radio to take up the space that had opened between them following Alex's confession. He pulled up in front of her hotel.

"Kelly, listen," he began. "I won't know much of anything until I talk with Charisse. And after I do, I will tell you what happened, no matter what it is."

"Are you in love with her?" She stared at her hands folded in her lap.

"No."

"You're not obligated to tell me anything. It's your life and your business. You and I are..."

"Are what?"

"Friends. That's it. Two friends taking things one day at a time."

He tugged on his bottom lip with his teeth. "I was hoping that we could be more than that."

She turned and looked at him. "Life is a bitch that way. Most times we get what we deserve not what we want." She unlocked the door and started to get out.

"Kelly..."

She glanced at him over her shoulder as she maneuvered her crutches.

"Let me help you upstairs."

"I'm pretty sure I can manage. Good night, Alex." She got out and went inside.

Alex sat there for several minutes until the doorman advised him that he couldn't stay there. Finally he pulled off and headed home. On the way he thought about going to Charisse's place and straightening this whole mess out.

How could this have happened? They'd been careful, at least he had. Every time he was with Charisse he'd used protection to prevent this very same scenario. Kids were not in his plans, at least not now, and certainly not with a woman that he wasn't in love with. They'd talked about it and she'd agreed.

They said the only foolproof prevention against pregnancy was abstinence or sterilization. He guessed they were right. What was equally unsettling about the whole debacle was Kelly's reaction, her sudden indifference. Although he could understand, he'd hoped that she would have…oh hell, he didn't know. If he'd been in her shoes he probably would have done and said the same things.

He wanted her to understand, be patient until he worked things out. But he had a feeling that she wouldn't. She was probably wondering what other tricks he was going to pull out of his hat.

Ultimately, in the end, Charisse held all the cards. And until she showed her hand there was nothing much he could do. If it came to it, he would face his responsibilities. He silently prayed that it wouldn't be a decision that would be forced upon him.

He made a quick right turn. This couldn't wait until tomorrow, and if Charisse wasn't at home, he'd wait until she returned.

Chapter 32

Charisse hung up from leaving a message on Stephanie's house phone. She debated about calling her cell phone and finally decided against it. No telling what she may be interrupting if she did that.

She went into her bathroom and stripped then turned on the shower and stepped in under the hot, beating water. What would she ultimately do if Alex decided that he didn't want to "do the right thing"? Would she be able to go through with a clinic visit or become another single mother statistic?

She rubbed her hand across her still flat stomach and the image of Alex and Kelly Maxwell smiling and laughing together flashed in her head. How close were they and for how long? Was she the reason why Alex broke things off with her? She found that hard to believe. Kelly Maxwell may be someone important in the sports world, but she certainly didn't appear to be the type Alex would go for. But apparently neither was she.

She finished up her shower and was drying off when she heard the doorbell ring. She took her robe from the hook on the back of the bathroom door and slipped it on. The bell rang again. She went to the front foyer and pressed the intercom.

"Who is it?"

"Alex. Can I come up?"

Charisse hesitated for a moment. She pressed the door to let him in.

"Thanks for letting me come up," Alex said as she stood in her doorway.

Charisse stepped aside to let him in, holding her robe a bit tighter around her body. Alex walked past her and into the living room where they'd spent many an evening together. Charisse shut the door and followed him inside. She stood in the center of the room with her arms folded.

"Well, you're here, I guess for a reason."

Alex sat down on her chocolate brown leather sofa, leaned forward, resting his arms on his thighs. He looked up at her. "I didn't want to wait until tomorrow to talk."

She lifted her chin but held her tongue.

"Have you thought about what you want to do?"

At least he didn't question whether or not it was his. "I've been thinking of nothing else since I found out."

"How long have you known?"

"Three weeks."

He blinked several times. "How far along are you?"

She slowly crossed the room and sat down. "Eight weeks."

His eyes widened. As much or as little as he knew about

pregnancy she was about as close as she could get to termination if that's what she decided to do.

"Eight weeks," he repeated. He ran his tongue across his dry lips, lowered his head and took a deep breath. "Whatever you decide to do...I'll stick by you."

"I'm bowled over by your enthusiasm."

"It's kinda hard for me to be enthusiastic about something I had no plans on happening."

"Neither did I, Alex," she snapped. She spun away from him to keep from crying. "I don't want anything from you."

"What's that supposed to mean?"

"Exactly what I said. I'm a big girl. I can handle this alone."

"That's not going to happen. Whatever you decide to do, I'm part of it, too."

"And what about your new girlfriend? Is she as amenable as you?"

"This has nothing to do with Kelly."

She turned to face him. "Is she the reason you left me?"

"No."

She pursed her lips. "I thought we had something, Alex." Her voice broke. "I really thought we did."

"You wanted something from me that I wasn't ready to offer."

"But you're willing to offer it to her?" she shot back.

"I don't know. We haven't committed to anything."

She gave a nasty laugh. "Isn't that just like you, not wanting to commit. How long do you think you can run in and out of people's lives and discard them at will when you become bored or tired or they want something more than great sex and a movie?"

"That's not fair." He stood, the lines in his brow creasing

into deep furrows. "You knew the deal going in. I never lied to you, never!"

"But sometimes Alex, those of us with a heart forget the rules, you know." She swallowed hard over the knot in her throat. "Maybe you should leave. I appreciate your interest and your concern." She started for the door and opened it. She turned to him. "If I find that I need you for anything I'll give you a call."

Alex got up from the couch and came toward her. They stood almost eye to eye. "I'm sorry. I wish things could have been different."

"Just go," she said, sounding worn out and defeated. "Just go."

He lowered his head and walked out.

The instant she closed the door she broke down and cried.

Kelly was stretched out across her bed, staring up at the ceiling. She should have known that Alex Hutchinson was too good to be true: handsome, intelligent, a doctor and he liked her. Boy, what a crock.

She turned onto her side. But everyone had baggage, she reasoned. She was a perfect example. When she laid her life story out on the table Alex didn't flinch, he didn't blink. Instead he wanted to know how he could help, insisted that she could do this, beat it and be a better person for it. She on the other hand was ready to catch the next plane back to Atlanta and the hell with it when he dropped his bomb.

In the midst of it all she had to admit that Alex was a decent guy. The first thing he'd said to her was that he was going to do the right thing, and she believed him. There were plenty of things he could have said, none of which would have been endearing but he didn't. The least she could do was give him the benefit of the doubt.

She reached over and picked up the phone. She had yet to return David's phone calls and really wasn't in the frame of mind to explain her whereabouts. She held the phone in her hand for a moment then punched in the numbers.

Alex answered on the second ring.

"If we're going to do this," she said, without preamble, "let's do it right."

"What do you suggest?"

"Tomorrow is a new day. Let's start from there."

"Are you sure?"

"As sure as I can be. If you stay honest with me, I'll stay honest with you."

He laughed with relief. "That's a great start."

Chapter 33

In the ensuing weeks Kelly and Alex spent as much time together as their schedules would allow. He picked her up from her rehab sessions and took her to her classes. In the evenings they shared dinner, went to movies and attended the concert that he'd promised.

Kelly had never been happier. Her ankle was healing, she'd gone from crutches to a cane, she was controlling her stress level, she hadn't binged in weeks and she was falling hard for Alex.

They were leaving the Blue Note jazz club in the West Village one Friday night just as the heavens opened up.

"One of these days I'm going to listen to the weatherman," Alex said as they ducked under the shelter of an overhang.

"We can't stay here forever and it doesn't look like it's going to let up anytime soon."

"The car is two blocks away. We'll get drenched and you

can't exactly run for it." He peeked out from beneath their cover. "You stay here. I'll go get the car and bring it back." He stepped out and she grabbed his arm.

"If you can get wet, so can I." She smiled up at him.

He looked at her for a moment and from the expression of determination on her face, he knew if he tried to leave without her, she would only follow him.

"All right." He took off his jacket and draped it over her head and shoulders. "Let's do this."

By the time they'd reached the garage where he'd parked the car, they were giddy with laughter and soaked to the skin.

"I'll have you home in no time so that you can get out of those wet clothes," Alex assured Kelly as he pulled out of the garage and into traffic.

"It's really coming down," she breathed, wiping water from her face.

"You really hung with me," Alex teased. "How's the ankle feeling?"

She gently massaged her lower leg. "Not bad actually."

"Good. You should probably soak it when you get in."

She nodded. "I will."

"How'd you like the show?"

She beamed with delight. "It was incredible. I've listened to Ashford and Simpson for years on the radio but to be less than ten feet away from them...wow." She shook her head in awe. "I never knew that they wrote for so many other artists."

"Yeah, how 'bout that. They wrote for all the major singers."

"It must be really interesting to be with someone for so many years and have a common bond like that and both of you absolutely love the same thing and work at it together."

"It takes work and determination to hold a relationship together. Both people have to want it as much as the other."

"Seeing a couple like that who are still together after all these years gives me hope," Alex said.

"Hope?"

"Yeah, that one day I'll have the same thing." He glanced at her.

"You really want the traditional wife, 2.5 kids and the white picket fence?"

He chuckled. "Quiet as it's kept I'm a traditional guy at heart. Don't get me wrong, I've loved my freedom, the great women that I've shared parts of my life with. But at some point, I'd like to put all the running behind me."

"How do you think that will change if…Charisse decides to keep the baby?"

Alex brought the car to stop in front of her hotel. "I'll have to find a way to deal with it, and make sure that my child has a place in whatever life I wind up living."

"You wouldn't marry her?" she pressed, needing to know the answers.

He put the car in park, unfastened his seatbelt and turned in his seat to look right at her. "One thing I do know and will always believe, a marriage is between two people who love each other, who have the same goals and values. I'm not in love with Charisse. I never was and to marry her because of this child would be the worst thing for the both of us. If she decides to go through with it, I'll be there for her and the child all the way, but marriage…" He shook his head.

She appreciated his honesty, she thought as he helped her out of the car. But was she ready for baby mama drama? Charisse and the baby would be an integral part of their lives for the rest of their lives—if she and Alex decided to pursue a relationship together. But she'd really grown to care about Alex and the kind of man that he was. She wasn't sure if she was ready to toss it all aside—at least not just yet.

She turned to him when they reached the front door of the hotel. "Do you want to come up for a little while—dry out?"

"If you don't mind a little wet company." He smiled.

"Not at all."

"Try to make yourself comfortable." Kelly said. "I'll get you a towel." She left to go into the bathroom.

Alex went to the bar and fixed them a drink while he waited.

"Here you go." She handed him a towel and he gave her the drink.

"Hope rum and Coke is good," he said, taking the towel and wiping his face.

"Perfect." She took a sip then put it down on the counter. "I'm going to change. Sorry I don't have anything to fit you."

"I'll be okay."

"Actually," she remembered. "There is a terry robe in the guest bathroom. You can put that on and I can call room service to take your wet things and get them dried." She opened the door to the adjoining suite and took the robe from the hook in the bathroom then brought it out to him.

"Thanks."

"You can change back there." She pointed in the direction she'd come from.

He nodded and headed off to change.

While he was gone, Kelly called room service then disconnected the hotel phone. The last thing she wanted was a call from David, checking up on her. By the time Alex returned with damp clothes in hand, room service was knocking on the door.

"I'll take those," she said. Alex handed her the clothes and she went to the door. "Can you get these dried for me?"

"Of course Ms. Maxwell. They should be ready in about an hour."

"Thank you." She closed the door and turned around. Her breath stopped short in her chest. When she looked at Alex she knew he had next to nothing on beneath that robe. Her mind went on a quick, wild excursion.

"You really should soak that ankle," he said, cutting into her fantasy.

"Oh, yes, I should."

"Why don't you sit down and put your foot up. I can take care of it for you. Just tell me where everything is."

"There's a basin under the sink in the bathroom."

"Be right back." He pointed a finger at her. "Now sit."

"Yes, Doc."

Kelly went into her bedroom and changed her wet clothes. She put on a long skirt and T-shirt and returned to the living room. Hearing Alex in the next room felt so comfortable and so right as if he always belonged there. She sat down on the couch and stretched out with her drink, feeling utterly content.

"Hope it's not too hot," Alex said returning with the basin of water. He came over to the couch and set the basin on the floor. "You look relaxed." He smiled.

"I am," she said in a dreamy voice.

He stared at her for a moment, all sorts of warm thoughts running through his head. He cleared his throat. "Uh, let's get that ankle in the water before it gets cold."

She lifted her leg and gently swung it over the side. Alex

took it in his hands and unfastened the Velcro strips on the brace. She drew in a deep breath when his warm fingers came in contact with her bare skin. He glanced up at her. Their eyes met as his fingers gently massaged her leg then put her foot in the warm waters.

"How does that feel?"

"Wonderful." Her eyes drifted closed.

He massaged her foot in the water, running strong fingers along her instep, up her ankle and calf—up and down, up and down. Kelly moaned softly and leaned further back against the pillows.

"Yes, right there," she sighed when his thumbs pressed against the insides of her calves.

His eyes rose up her legs. She reached down and took his hands raising them higher up her leg until his hands embraced her thigh.

"It's all right," she whispered.

His eyes met hers. He rose up on his knees. She held her breath. The pads of his thumbs were at her waist, rising slowly to the underside of her breasts.

"Are you sure?"

She nodded her head. He got on the couch next to her and took her face in his hands. He leaned forward until his mouth was inches away from hers.

"Kiss me," she urged.

And he did, slow and tender as if she would break. Blood rushed to her head and she felt warm all over. She wrapped her arms around him, pulling him close. He reached behind her and loosened the clip that held her hair in place letting it fall in waves around her face and shoulders.

He kissed her cheeks, her neck, slipping down to the crests of her breasts as his hands eased beneath her shirt.

She drew in a sharp breath when his fingers toyed with her nipples that grew hard beneath his touch.

With a sudden urgency he leaned back and pulled her shirt over her head.

"I want to see you." He unfastened her bra and marveled at her beauty before taking one firm nipple in his mouth, his tongue playing maddening games with it.

Kelly's head spun. Her body shuddered as waves of pleasure coursed through her. She pulled his robe away from his shoulders, baring his chest, and ran her hands along his warm taut skin, memorizing every inch.

Alex left one breast and went to the other then let his mouth trail down her stomach. She moaned in delight as her stomach quivered from the tiny nips from his teeth. He fumbled with the front button of her skirt. She pushed his hands away and undid the button then pushed the skirt down over her hips.

He leaned away from her, his eyes running up and down her near nude body.

"You are so perfect," he said. And when he said it, she believed it. She felt beautiful.

Alex stood then reached down and lifted her into his arms, cradling her like a baby. "Not here," he said, kissing and nibbling her as he walked toward her bedroom.

Once inside he gently placed her on the bed and unfastened the belt of his robe letting it drop to the floor before he joined her. For a moment he laid on his side, facing Kelly, simply taking her all in, stroking her body with his hands and eyes.

She reached up and caressed his cheek, a soft smile of invitation framing her mouth. She moved closer to him and felt his erection press against her thigh. She wanted to feel him, totally. She took him in her hand and stroked him feeling him pulse and throb in her grasp. His soft groans of pleasure only stirred her own rapidly rising longing. She drew his mouth to hers, her tongue dancing erotically with his.

"You can't keep that up," he hissed from between his teeth.

"Like it?" she taunted.

"Almost too much." He eased her onto her back until he was above her. He kissed her long and deep holding on to those moments of prelude for as long as he could. He wanted to remember it all, every touch, every breath, every sigh.

Kelly shifted her body beneath him until he rested between her thighs. His erection pressed right up against the wetness of her folds and she moaned with anticipation instinctively raising her hips against him.

Alex grabbed her hips in his hands and rose up on his knees. "Look at me."

Kelly opened her eyes and when she did Alex pushed inside her as deeply as her body would allow. Her back arched and a cry caught and held in her throat.

For a moment, he didn't move giving them a moment to experience the newness of their union. Then nature took over and he began to move slow and steady, in and out of her.

Kelly wrapped herself around him, not wanting an inch of space to separate them. The sensations that Alex created in her body left her breathless and she wanted to absorb them all. His hands and mouth were everywhere. Her body was on fire. He whispered in her ear, telling her how wonderful she felt, what she was doing to him, how good it was. Her head spun.

"Oh, girl," he groaned. "Just like that."

She rotated her hips. "Like that?"

He looked down at her with a smile of delight on his face. "Yeah, like that."

She felt like liquid fire, he thought as the powerful sensations rolled through him. He wanted it to last all night long but if she kept doing what she was doing to him it would be over soon. He didn't want it to stop.

It was more exquisite than she'd imagined, more intense. Alex was making love to her, to her body and her mind. That had never happened to her before. His every touch ignited a new thrill that rushed through her. And his tender words of adoration kept the fire lit. She wanted to give him her best, all of her. She wanted to make him feel as incredible as she did.

Then a warm tingling sensation began in her feet, shimmied up her legs, her thighs, played havoc in the center of her stomach and shot to her head only to reverse course and build with intensity in her pelvis. Her insides began to quake with every move Alex made. She whimpered helplessly as her entire body became one exposed nerve and the shock waves of bliss had her dizzy, crying out for more, yet needing to be released from the sweet torture.

"Come to me, baby," Alex whispered in her ear, as he thrust in and out of her, each move building with urgency.

"Hutch!" She dug her nails into his back as white light popped behind her eyes and her body shuddered as if electrified with volts of joy.

The muscles in his back snapped, freezing his spine as the powerful pulls of her insides sucked him in and sent him over the edge.

His full weight pressed her down as he buried his face

in her neck, humming softly against her hot flesh. Slowly she lowered her legs and held him in her arms.

"I didn't expect that," he finally said.

"Neither did I." The soul-stirring interlude replayed in her mind and body as it began contracting again.

He felt her need and his own grew in response. This time he moved slow and deliberate, deep and long, carving out his place in her body.

Kelly whimpered helplessly, her body no longer her own, but his to pleasure as he pleased.

He cupped her breasts, kneading them as he moved within her, setting off another flurry of delight.

They lay entwined with each other, their hearts beating in unison. Kelly closed her eyes then forced them open wanting to assure herself that it wasn't all a dream. She stroked his back, feeling the muscles flex beneath her fingertips. She smiled. It was real. She closed her eyes and drifted off to a bliss-filled sleep, secure in Alex's embrace.

When he awoke it was nearly two a.m.

"Oh man," Alex groaned, peeking at the digital clock on the nightstand. He tried to sit up but Kelly was fast asleep nestled in his arms. He kissed the top of her head. "Wake up sleepyhead."

She mumbled something unintelligible and snuggled closer. Alex laughed. "I gotta go, sweetheart. I need to get home. I have surgery in the morning."

"Hmm," she mumbled and slowly opened her eyes. "What time is it?"

"Ten after two."

She sat up and stretched. "Are you sure?" She peeped at the clock. "You really don't have to leave you know. The hotel took care of your clothes." Her eyes widened in alarm. "Your clothes! They probably brought them back and we didn't even hear them."

She started to get up.

"You can stay put. I'll go check." He got out of bed and went into the front room.

She heard the door open then close. Alex returned with clothes in hand.

"Now this is what I call service. They had them cleaned, pressed and hanging on a rack in front of the door."

"Well since your hospital skills are in your head and not your apartment," she said and yawned, "you can come back to bed. I can have the front desk arrange for a wake-up call so you won't oversleep."

He hung the clothes up on the top of door and came to the bed. He looked down at her, the full length of her naked body drawing him like a magnet.

"I can't guarantee that there will be much sleeping going on if I get back in that bed with you."

She raised her arms to welcome him. "Is that a threat or a promise?"

"Both."

"I like the sound of that," she whispered.

Alex crawled in bed next to her to pick up where they'd never left off.

"Do you have a class today?" Alex asked as he stepped out of the shower toweling his face and hair.

"No, not today."

"Want to do something later? Maybe I'll fix dinner for us at my place."

She beamed then frowned. "Can you cook?"

"Let's put it this way, I won't starve to death and I haven't poisoned anyone yet."

"That's mildly reassuring."

He put on his shirt and buttoned it. "I take that as a yes?"

"Sure. I'm game. What time?"

"Hmm. I have a long day today. Surgery, clinic and grand rounds at the hospital. I should be off around five. Let's say I pick you up around seven-thirty."

"I'll be ready."

He put on his pants and shoes. "How do I look?" he said with a wicked grin.

"Not bad for a man who couldn't find his way home last night."

He crossed the room to where she was curled on her side of the bed. "Oh I found my way home, all right." He leaned down and kissed her. "It was beautiful," he said looking into her eyes.

"My sentiments exactly."

He stepped back and smiled at her. "I'll see you later. I don't know if I'll get a chance to call, but if I can I will."

"Okay, but don't worry about it."

"See you later."

After Alex left for work, Kelly dozed off for another hour or so. When she awoke it was a little after ten and she was famished. Easing out of the bed she reached for the phone to dial room service. She placed an order for a four-cheese omelet, hash browns, Canadian ham, wheat toast, orange juice and coffee. As she hung up the phone it hit her. Since she'd been seeing Alex she hadn't had any of her eating episodes and she'd had no desire to purge her food. A smile of astonishment moved across her face. She was sure that the counseling sessions helped, but more importantly her self-esteem was at an all-time high. She couldn't remember ever feeling good about herself and her prospective future. She'd always been at someone's mercy. And now she felt that she'd finally gained some control over her life; from the learning classes, the counseling and finding someone who genuinely cared about her for who she was, with all of her warts and flaws and not for what they could get out of it.

Alex was successful in his own right. He didn't need her name or notoriety to feel empowered. Never once did he feel "it was a good thing" to have a learning disability and that it was something she should ignore and hide from the world. He dared her to gain control over it and in turn control her life.

David fed on her weaknesses, her need to be protected. But she had been an enabler. No one can do to you what you don't allow them to do. For years she'd allowed David to control her life, her thoughts, her actions, until she was only a shadow of a person.

Maybe this accident was the best thing that could have happened to her. It opened her mind and her entire life up to endless possibilities. How many hundreds, thousands of men and women endured what she'd gone through over the years? Hiding in shame, finding a way to fake their way through life's daily routines. Or worse, not knowing that what they were dealing with could be helped so that they could function more fully in society.

All she'd ever wanted was a chance to be like everyone else, to feel worthy and valued as a person not as some athletic icon, some illusion. Sure, running had been her salvation over the years. Without it, there's no telling where she would have wound up. For that, she would always be grateful to David. But now it was her time at life, to live it as she saw fit. Even if she could never run again she knew she'd find a way to survive.

She'd been toying with an idea for the past few days and she was going to make it happen. But until she researched it further and the final diagnosis was given about her ankle she would keep it to herself.

Her stomach grumbled in anticipation when she heard noise at the front door. She got out of bed and went to the front door just as it opened.

"David."

Chapter 34

"Don't you look like the cat that ate the canary," Ruby commented as she and Alex walked down the hospital corridors.

"And you sound like you're on a fishing expedition," he said, ducking the comment.

"Fine, don't tell me what's going on. By the grin on your face and that look of delight in your eyes, I can figure it out on my own. You slept with her didn't you?"

"Must you know everything?"

"Yes."

Alex pressed the button for the elevator. He glanced at her and shoved his hands in the pockets of his lab coat. "For your information…it's none of your business."

She pursed her lips in annoyance. "Just like I thought. Well I hope you know what you're doing. That's all I can say."

"I'm sure it's not all you can say."

They stepped onto the elevator and held their conversation away from the ears of the other passengers. They got out on the second floor and walked to Alex's office.

"It was worth it," he said when they stepped inside and closed the door. He rounded the desk and sat down then looked up at Ruby.

"I hear a but. So what is it?" She sat down, too.

He heaved a sigh. "We were out a couple of weeks ago, me and Kelly and we ran into Charisse."

Ruby's eyes widened but she reserved her comments.

"She uh, told me she's pregnant."

"What! Hutch how in the hell did you let that happen?"

"I didn't let anything happen. I was careful every time."

She slowly shook her head.

"So I went by her place that night after I dropped Kelly off—to talk." He paused. "Basically, I still don't know what she plans to do. I told her whatever decision she makes that I would stick by her and the baby. She pretty much told me that she doesn't want anything from me."

"Whew. Did you tell Kelly…before or after you slept with her?"

"Before. I wanted to be up-front with her. I told her the same night that Charisse told me."

"And what did she say?"

"She said that she still wanted to work things out between the two of us."

Ruby arched and lowered a brow. "At least she made some kind of informed decision. And you haven't spoken to Charisse since then?"

"No."

"You do realize that you are going to be tied to this woman and the child for the rest of your natural life."

"Yeah, yeah, I know. If things could be different they

would be, but they aren't. I'm not in love with Charisse. And I'm not going to be married to someone I'm not in love with. Whatever the baby needs, he or she will have. Period."

"Well, you've gotten yourself into some fixes before but this one..." Her words trailed off. She frowned as the thought hit her. "You've known this for weeks and didn't say a word to me about it?"

"I knew you would flip and I really wasn't up to feeling you ripping me a new one."

"You're right about that." She was thoughtful for a moment. "I know you really want to hear my opinion so I'm going to give it to you."

"Hmm," he grumbled.

"Even if Charisse hasn't contacted you, don't you think you should try to reach her? The last thing you want is a surprise. You can't sit back and let things happen around you. Being a woman, I know that even if she says she doesn't want you around, she doesn't mean it. You may not be in love with her, but I don't think she felt the same way. Right about now she's probably scared and confused as all hell and feeling pretty alone in all this."

"You're right. But she practically kicked me out of the door."

"What did you expect her to do?"

"I'll call her. Today."

Ruby stood. "Do that. Well, I have patients waiting. I'll catch up with you later." She turned to leave then stopped. "And Hutch..."

"Yes."

She smiled. "I'm glad you're happy and I really hope that things work out for you and Kelly."

"Thanks, Ruby. That means a lot coming from you."

She walked out, leaving Alex alone to wrestle with his thoughts.

"No time like the present," he murmured and picked up the phone.

"Charisse Clark. How may I help you?"

"Charisse it's Alex."

There was a moment of silence before she spoke. "How are you?"

"Okay. Concerned about you."

"I'm fine."

"Are you?"

"Yes, actually, I am, Alex. My conscience is clear. I've had time to think and I feel secure with my decision."

His heart thumped in his chest.

"And what decision have you come to?"

"I'm not going through with it."

"Are you sure?"

"I think it's the best thing. I don't want my child to grow up with a part-time father and that's all you could ever be."

He wasn't sure if he was relieved or saddened by her decision. "Charisse…"

"There's really nothing for you to say, Alex. It's my body and my decision. I appreciate your concern but I don't need it. Really I don't."

"I want to be there for you, Charisse."

"That's not necessary. Listen, I'd love to chat but I have a meeting in five minutes. Take care, Alex." She disconnected the call before he had a chance to respond.

Absently he hung up the phone. This was what he wanted wasn't it? Then why did he feel so utterly crappy?

"What are you doing here?"

David gave her a hard look and walked past her. He

strode in, tossed his carry-all in the corner and turned to face her.

"How long have you been seeing Alex Hutchinson behind my back?"

She put her hands on her hips and glared at him. "What?"

"How long, Kelly?"

"Is that why you came all the way back from Atlanta? And who told you that anyway?"

"What difference does it make who told me," he fired back thinking about his conversation with Stephanie and her revelations from her cousin. "It's a small world. Let's put it that way."

Kelly slammed the door and came into the front room. "First of all, David, let's get one thing straight and out of the way. I'm a grown woman. I can do as I please and see whom I please whenever I please."

"Is that right. Well I wonder how confident you'll feel when I sue that fucking hospital for a breach of ethics!"

"You wouldn't dare."

"Wouldn't I? Don't bet me."

"Alex isn't breaching any ethics. He's no longer my doctor."

"What!" David's eyes flashed as if hit with lightning. "Since when? Why wasn't I told? I was the one who got him as your doctor."

She folded her arms in defiance. "It's done. I'm seeing the chief of staff."

David fumed with outrage, pacing the floor like a caged animal. He spun toward her. "You're coming back to Atlanta. I knew I should have never left you here."

"I'm not going anywhere."

"What?"

"You heard me. I'm not going anywhere. My rehab is coming along fine. I'm in a relationship that I'm happy with and I'm not leaving." She paused. "And I'm taking classes."

His brow creased into a scowl. "Classes? What are you talking about?"

She sat down and calmly told him about her learning classes, leaving out the counseling sessions that she was also attending for her eating problem.

David opened his mouth but no words would come out. He sat down as if he'd been pricked by a pin and deflated.

"I'm tired of feeling like I'm handicapped. I want to, need to be able to rely on myself."

"I've always been there for you Kelly. I've taken care of you since day one."

"I know and I appreciate everything that you've done for me. But I must do this for myself. You need to understand that. You taking care of me all these years, reading for me, standing in for me, handling my finances, my life...all that did was make my dependence on you worst. It didn't help me. It kept me a cripple."

"I did it for you."

"But now I need to do it for me. Me, David."

He snickered. "He put this craziness in your head didn't he? What are all of your fans, the media going to say if they find out? I've protected you all these years."

"I'll deal with that when the time comes. And when it does, I'll tell them. I'm dyslexic. I've had a reading problem since I was a little girl that was never treated. And now I'm learning how to learn all over again." When she said the words out loud they somehow gave her a sense of freedom, of pride as if she'd been released from the chains that bound her.

A million thoughts tumbled through his head at once.

For years he'd kept Kelly bound to him with her secret. He'd virtually released her from any responsibility for her own life in order to benefit himself and the team. Without that hold, without her need for him...

"Look, if this is what you want, fine. You shall have it. I've never kept you from doing what you wanted." He stood. "But from now on, you're on your own. Totally."

He picked up his bag. "Preliminaries start in three weeks. If you're not ready, you will be cut from the team. There are three major endorsement deals on my desk for you awaiting signature, contingent upon you being able to perform. If you're not back and ready to go your contract will be cancelled." He smirked. "There was a little clause in your contract that stipulated that should you become incapacitated during the training season, your contract and any advances you were paid would be cancelled and the monies returned with the ongoing interest. Guess you didn't read the fine print. Not to mention the sponsors and advertisers that are going to be really pissed off if you aren't ready."

Kelly was breathing hard and fast. Her hands shook as she listened to the sentence he was gleefully inflicting upon her.

He walked toward the door relishing the stunned look of disbelief on her face. "You see Kelly, those are the little things that I could have protected you from should it have come down to this. It wouldn't have been a problem. But now that you don't need me anymore, I suppose you'll have to figure it all out for yourself."

He opened the door. "Good luck."

For what seemed like an eternity Kelly sat frozen in place. She couldn't believe what he'd said. But in her gut she knew every word of it was true.

Chapter 35

When Alex arrived to pick Kelly up from her class she was unusually quiet.

"You want to tell me what's bugging you?" he finally asked after riding around in virtual silence.

"After you left this morning, David showed up."

The news so stunned him he nearly hit the car in front of him and had to squeeze the brakes. "David showed up? Did you know he was coming?"

"I had no idea."

"Is he still here."

"No. After he gave me his ultimatum he left."

"Ultimatum? What do you mean?"

She told him what was said and the predicament she was in.

"Shit."

"My sentiments exactly." She sighed heavily. "I spoke

to Dr. Logan today. He said that I should be ready to go back in time for preliminaries but I would have to continue with rehab therapy in Atlanta."

His stomach knotted. "So you'll be leaving."

She glanced at him. "Of course. I have a life in Atlanta. And it's more important than ever that I get back and straighten things out. I need to look over my contracts and they are in Atlanta." She frowned and touched his arm. "Hutch?"

He shook his head. "I guess there was a part of me that stupidly believed that you would stay."

"I can't. Too much is at stake. My entire life, my reputation is on the line. David has manipulated me enough over the years. I can't sit back and let him run over me now."

"Of course. You're right." He looked at her. "Sounds as if you're going to need a lawyer as well, if what he says about the contract is true."

"I know." She was thoughtful for a moment. "You did say that Atlanta was a great place to visit," she said softly.

He brought the car to a stop in front of her hotel. He turned and looked at her while taking her hand in his. "And it's an even greater place to visit since I know you'll be there. And there's always the off-season. You can spend it in New York."

"This will certainly be a long distance relationship." She smiled.

He leaned over and tenderly kissed her. "We'll find a way to make it work."

She looked into his eyes. "Something else is on your mind. Tell me."

He took a breath. "I talked with Charisse today."

Her heart knocked in her chest. "Oh. And?"

"She told me she doesn't plan to go through with the pregnancy."

Kelly lowered her head. "I'm sorry." She looked up and at him. "How do you feel about that?"

"Mixed. A part of me is relieved, another part disappointed."

"Disappointed in what way?"

"That things couldn't have worked out differently. That the woman who was carrying a child of mine would be someone I was totally in love with and it was something that we both wanted. Life is sacred. I don't want any part of taking away from it. Ya know."

"Do you think she's making the right decision?"

"It's the right decision for her. I can't force her to do what she doesn't want to do."

They were silent for a moment, each lost in thought.

Finally Kelly spoke. "One thing I've learned is that truth is always revealed and we each find a way to deal with the cards that we're given. You need to search your heart and soul and decide what you want for you. It's just like you told me. You can't let anyone else have control over your life. It leaves you powerless. And trust me, from one who knows, it's not a great feeling."

He turned to her and grinned. "How'd you get so wise?"

"I have a great teacher." She gave him a quick peck on the lips. "Speaking of teaching, I have some work to go over for my class tomorrow. Are you coming up for a little while?"

"You sure I won't be a distraction?" he asked with a wicked glint in his eyes.

"Didn't you hear? I'm a quick study. I know exactly what to do with distractions." She winked and got out of the car.

* * *

"So when do you plan to go back to Atlanta?" he asked when Kelly finally put her study guides away for the evening.

"As soon as Dr. Logan gives me the okay. I'm off the cane as of today. And he's going to start me on the treadmill tomorrow to build up my strength. But he said the X-rays look great. The break is completely healed. I just need to gain my mobility back."

Alex nodded. "And you're sticking with the nutrition plan and the supplements?"

"Yes, Doc." She chuckled. "And I haven't been bingeing and purging in weeks."

"Excellent. So you think the counseling is really helping?"

She came and snuggled next to him on the bed. "I know it is. I'm staying centered, dealing with my daily issues one day at a time. Trying not to overdo it. And you're a big help, too."

"Me?" he asked, trying to sound surprised.

"Yes, you." She nudged him in the ribs.

"I don't think I would have taken these steps without you." She looked up at him.

"You would have in time. There is a fighter spirit in you. All it needed was a chance to come out."

"Well, thank you for giving it a shove."

"For you…anything." He lowered his head and kissed her softly and tenderly. He ran his fingers through her unbound hair. "The world is yours for the taking, sweetheart. And I know nothing is going to stand in your way."

"I want you to be there for the ride."

"Do you?"

"Yes."

"I'd like nothing better."

She pressed her lips to his, drawing on his warmth and strength, relishing in the feel of his body so close to hers. She needed to be sure that the exquisite sensations she'd felt the night before were not imagined, she thought as she slowly unbuttoned his shirt.

Her fingers trailed across his chest reacquainting herself with the texture of his skin, the feel of his mouth against her lips, her neck, reliving the electric currents that rippled up and down her spine when he caressed her breasts.

She moaned in delight when he loosened the tie on her sweatpants and his probing, talented fingers found their way into her panties to taunt her clit until it was hard and throbbing, sending shivers of longing running through her veins. She gasped when his finger slid up inside her, and pleasured her long and slow.

Her thigh muscles tightened as he kept up the teasing, faster, slower, faster, then back to her clit, then in and out again. Her heart was racing so fast she could barely breathe.

Alex moved away from her and she shuddered, instantly missing the thrill of his touch. He pulled her pants and panties off and tossed them on the floor then lifted her shirt over her head and unfastened her bra discarding them both. For a moment he let his eyes feast on her incredible body, soft, warm and hard in all the right places.

He started at her lips, then her neck then suckled each breast until she thought she'd faint. He trailed down her stomach, licking and nibbling her until he reached the dark warmth, the treasure between her thighs. His mouth nuzzled her there and she moaned with pleasure, but when his touch laved her swollen, pulsing clit she grabbed the sheets in a death grip and nearly sobbed.

His tender, probing exploration sent rivers of fire running through her. She shook, trembled, begged him to stop, to go on, to give her more, less...yes...no...Yes!!

"Ahhhh." Her body rocked and bucked as if electrified and Alex kept the pressure up until she was wilted and totally spent.

"You okay?" he whispered as she snuggled against him.

"I'll never be quite the same." She caressed his shoulders. "No one has ever..."

"Good, then I'm glad the first time was with me."

"Can it stay that way?"

"For as long as you want it."

He gathered her to him and held her close, wishing that moments like this would be untarnished. They both had issues to deal with, things that would change them, but as long as they stood firm and together they could beat the odds. That he was certain of.

Chapter 36

"You told him?" Charisse asked.

"Of course I told him." Stephanie examined her nails. "You wouldn't have said anything to me if you didn't want it to get back to him."

Charisse sat down on the side of the bed. "So what happened?"

"He was livid to say the least. I rarely see David out of control but he was definitely pissed. He'd been like a raging bull around the whole team. We were glad to get rid of him."

"Get rid of him. Why? What happened?"

"He got on a flight to New York this morning. Said he was going to straighten the whole thing out." She smiled. "And if I know David, Kelly will no longer be a problem for you and Alex. If, of course, that's what you really want."

Charisse closed her eyes and rubbed her forehead. The beginnings of another major headache loomed. They'd been coming more frequently lately. She attributed them to the personal stress that she was under.

"Well, aren't you going to say thank you?" Stephanie asked.

"Sorry. Thanks."

"Gee cuz, don't sound so enthused. Now you can go after your man full steam ahead with no obstacles."

"I decided not to go through with it."

"Humph, wish I would have known," she said, totally unmoved by the news. "I would have saved my little bombshell for some other time. Oh well."

"Listen I'm going to lie down. My head is killing me. Thanks for calling and for trying to help."

"Anytime, you know you can count on me. Take care and take something for that headache."

Charisse hung up. She knew Stephanie meant well, but her way of going about things were really out in left field. She was different somehow, more edgy, wired. Stephanie had always been the more gregarious of the two but this was a different element. Sometimes talking to her it was as if she no longer knew who she was.

She stretched out on the bed and shut her eyes praying that the pounding in her head would go away.

It was almost midnight by the time David's flight landed at Atlanta's Hatfield Airport. It had cost him a pretty penny to change his ticket and finagle his way onto a return flight at the last minute.

Maybe he should have stayed, he thought as he got in the taxi, and found a way to make Kelly see the light and break things off with the good doctor. Just the idea of the two of them together had him seeing red. But he'd have her back under control in short order or she would be ruined and she'd have no one to blame besides herself. His main goal now was a winning team. And he could have that with Stephanie.

Thinking about her made him hot. He knew it was foolish to get involved with her but he couldn't seem to shake her loose. He couldn't get enough of what she offered. It was like an addiction and every time they were together it was more mind-blowing than the last time. Her stamina was unbelievable.

"Driver, make a left at the next corner." He smiled to himself. A romp with Stephanie was just what he needed to take the edge off and his mind away from Kelly.

The taxi pulled up in front of Stephanie's town house. The lights were on. Good she was still up. David paid the driver and got out.

Before he could ring the front doorbell the door was pulled open. Stephanie stood in the frame with a long, off-white silk robe, partially opened. She had nothing on underneath.

"Why Coach Livingston, what a pleasant surprise." She licked her lips. "Is there something you needed?"

He stepped up to her and roughly grabbed her around the waist, pulling her hard up against him. "Yes," he said from between his teeth. He reached down between her legs. "This."

"Ooh, Coach, I think we should take this inside. We may cause a scene."

They stepped in and David kicked the door shut behind them.

After a rousing session, David and Stephanie lay back on her queen-size bed sipping wine.

"I really didn't expect you back so soon. You only left this morning," Stephanie said, draping her leg across both of his. She played with his earlobe.

"Took care of things sooner than I expected." He could never tell her or anyone about the kind of relationship that he and Kelly shared over the years, especially now that it was basically over. And now that she was determined to sever her ties with him.

"I'm sure she was surprised to see you."

He didn't respond.

"Well, was she?"

He pushed her leg off him and got up. "Does it matter?"

Stephanie sat up in the bed and stared at his back. "What happened between the two of you?"

"It doesn't concern you Stephanie."

"Doesn't concern me!" Her head snapped back as if she'd been slapped. She rose up on her knees. "I'm the woman you're sleeping with, the one you came straight back to." Her voice rose in pitch and volume. "I'm the one that told you what was going on with your precious, do no wrong Kelly. And now it doesn't concern me."

David spun around and was stunned by the wild look in her eyes. "Take it easy. And no it does not concern you. What went on between me and Kelly stays between me and Kelly. End of story."

Suddenly she sprung up from the bed and slapped him across his face. "You bastard. You slept with her didn't you!" She went at him with nails bared.

David grabbed her by the wrist and tried to push her back down on the bed but she fought him like a woman possessed.

"You're not going to do this to me! You're not going to treat me like this." She swung and kicked, screaming at the top of her lungs. She wrestled one hand free and scratched him across the face.

David howled. Her nails felt like razors. He put her in a headlock until she gasped for air. "Don't make me hurt you," he said, breathing hard.

Her eyes bulged as she struggled to breathe. Slowly he released her and eased up off the bed.

Stephanie grabbed her throat, stumbled to her feet and ran for the bathroom. David listened to the rushing water in the sink while he got dressed. She was crazy. He knew he shouldn't have gotten involved with her, but this was totally out of control. He had to put a stop to it and now.

She came out of the bathroom. Her eyes were red and even at the distance between them he could see the bruising around her neck.

He stood up. "Look." He ran his hand across his head. "This is not going to continue. I don't know what your problem is but—"

"My problem?" She tossed her head back and laughed. "I'm not the one with the problem, David. It's you. She has you so twisted you can't see straight." She stormed across the room and refilled her glass, downed the wine and refilled it again. She sniffed hard then turned to face him. "Did you sleep with her?" This time her question was more a plea than an accusation. She pressed her lips tightly together.

For a moment she looked incredibly vulnerable, David thought, as if she had warm blood running through her veins and really cared about someone other than herself. Not Stephanie Daniels. Don't even fall for it.

"No, I didn't. Satisfied?"

She lowered her head and actually looked sheepish. "I'm sorry," she whispered.

David knew he wasn't hearing right. Did Stephanie just apologize?

"Forget it. Look why don't you take a few days off from training. Relax."

She sniffed. "Yeah, sure." She turned away. "I'm tired."

David straightened, drew in a long breath. He walked up to her but she didn't turn around. He placed his hand on her shoulder. "I'm sorry about what happened tonight."

Stephanie nodded her head but didn't offer more of a response. She stood there until she heard the door shut.

He was not going to ignore her. She opened a new bottle of wine. He was not going to toss her aside for Kelly Maxwell. She wouldn't let it happen. She refilled her glass.

Chapter 37

"I was thinking about our talk yesterday," Kelly was saying as she stood at the sink brushing her teeth.

Alex leaned against the door frame of the bathroom, loving every minute of watching her walk around in the nude.

"What part?"

"The part about me going back to Atlanta."

"Oh."

"I really don't want to wait until I get the okay from Dr. Logan." She rinsed her mouth and turned around, resting her hip on the side of the sink.

"You can't be serious. There's no telling what damage you might do to your ankle if—"

"I didn't mean for good." She saw the lines of concern slip away from his tight expression. She smiled. "I thought I would go back for a couple of days just to get my papers together and come back. I want to finish my rehab here and

I want to continue with my classes. They'll be finished soon. And I want to stick with my counselor at least here until I can find someone back in Atlanta."

Alex nodded in understanding.

"I really want to go over my contracts and…I was hoping you would go over them with me."

"Of course. I can get my lawyer to take a look if you want."

"One step at a time. Okay?"

He held up his hand. "Okay, okay. I'm sorry. It's the man in me, just wants to jump in and fix it."

They laughed.

"So what do you think?"

He stepped up to her, reached out and wiped a spot of toothpaste away from the corner of her mouth. "I think I'm very proud of you." He slid his fingers through the back of her hair and drew her toward him. "And I think I'm falling in love with you."

She drew in a breath and it stuck for a moment in her chest. "When do you think you'll know for sure?" she asked slowly.

"One day at a time," he answered. "It becomes clearer and stronger one day at a time." He lowered his head and touched his lips to hers.

Kelly wrapped her arms around him and melted into his embrace, and silently hoped that the days came fast and furious.

"Do you have someone to meet you?" Alex asked as they drove to the airport two days later.

"I'll be fine. I'll take a cab to my house."

"I really wish I could go with you, but I have two surgeries this week."

"Stop worrying. I'll be fine."

"I just don't want you there alone. No telling how David is going to react when you see him."

"I can handle David."

"Call me when you arrive."

"I will."

He pulled up to the departure gate, got out and helped her with her bag.

Kelly grabbed his hand. "I don't want you to worry. I'm going to be fine and I'll be back before you know it."

"I know. And I promise to try not to worry."

"Good." She reached up and kissed him for a long moment. When she eased away she said, "There's more where that came from when I get back."

He grinned. "I'll be counting the hours."

She picked up her bag and slung it over her shoulder. "I think I'm falling in love with you, too, one day at a time." She turned and walked into the terminal before he could respond.

Alex stood on the curb for several moments trying to keep her in sight for as long as possible until the crowd swallowed her up.

Reluctantly he got back in his car, her parting words reverberating in his head. Things were going to work out between them. He felt it in his gut. Yet, the sooner she got back the better he would feel.

The flight to Atlanta was pretty uneventful. Kelly spent most of it drifting in and out of a light sleep with images of her and Alex making for pleasant dreams. When she'd told him how she felt about him it was liberating. She'd never confessed that to anyone, never came close. Of course there were obstacles that they would have to overcome but she was willing and had walked into it with her eyes wide open.

Alex, though protective, didn't smother her or make her feel inadequate. If anything he wanted her empowered, to be as strong as she could be. That was important. It's what gave her the impetus to finally fight her inner battles and believe that she could win. No matter what happened between her and Alex from here on out, she would always be grateful to him for that.

Wow, she was in love. She smiled to herself. She didn't just think it, she knew it and she was loved back for the first time in her life.

When she departed the plane and went to the exit, she quickly donned her baseball cap and pulled it low over her brow. She may not be a readily recognizable face in the hustle and flow of New York, but her hometown of Atlanta was a different story. She wanted to get to her place and behind the sanctuary of her closed doors without being accosted by news hungry photographers.

When she stepped outside and back on familiar territory, she drew in a deep breath of warm southern air. It was good to be back. She made her way to the taxi line, waited her turn for the next available cab and before she knew it she was pulling up in front of her house.

Kelly went from room to room turning on lights and opening windows to air out the spaces. Once she had some circulation going, she went to her bedroom, took off her sneakers and put her feet up. She leaned down and massaged her ankle, pleased that it didn't ache and wasn't in the least bit swollen. What a relief.

She reached for the phone and it rang in her hand.

"Hello?"

"I didn't realize how much I was going to miss you until you were actually gone."

She leaned back against the stack of bed pillows and smiled.

"I hear missing a person is a good thing."

"Not from this end. How was your flight, baby?"

"Smooth for the most part. I slept the majority of the time. How did surgery go?"

"Good. Both of my patients will feel like new money in a few weeks."

She chuckled at the analogy. "Well, I just got in and aired the place out a little."

"So you haven't had a chance to get your papers together?"

"Actually they're not here."

"What do you mean? You keep them in a safety deposit box or something?"

"No." She hesitated. "David has all of the contracts."

He spewed out an expletive and Kelly cringed.

"I wish you would have told me that before you left, Kelly. I would have moved hell and high water to be there with you."

"It will be fine. I promise."

He blew out a breath. "I don't like it. But there isn't much that I can do about it from here. You just hurry up and take care of your business so you can come back here."

"Yes, sir." She giggled.

"Very funny." He paused. "This afternoon…when you left…did you mean what you said at the airport?"

"Every word," she said without hesitation.

"Yeah, me, too," he said.

"So it's official. We both think we're in love!"

Alex laughed along with her.

"And we are going to work real hard testing to find out if it's the real thing."

"I like the sound of that."

"Me, too. Listen, get some rest and we'll talk tomorrow. Okay?"

"Absolutely." She yawned. "I'll give you a call in the afternoon when I think you're done at the clinic."

"Cool. How's the ankle?"

"Great. Feels really good. No swelling, no tenderness."

"Excellent. You'll be back on the track in no time."

"It's looking real good."

"Well, good night, babe. Talk to you tomorrow."

"Good night." Thoughtfully she hung up the phone, a smile of pure contentment sat on her face. This love thing was truly wonderful and she wanted more of it.

Since Alex beat her to the punch with the phone call, she could relax. She went in the bathroom and ran the tub, humming to herself as she did. Life was looking really good to her.

Her life and her expectations for herself had changed dramatically since she'd met Alex. She felt confident about herself for the first time in her life. She was no longer terrified of not being able to run again. She finally understood that she was so much more than Kelly Maxwell the athlete. But her prominent status in the world of sports would serve her well with her plans. And she planned to capitalize on her name and notoriety.

Chapter 38

"When do you think Stephanie will be back?" Herb asked David.

David shut the drawer of his desk. "I told her to take a couple of days off. She needed the break. She's been working really hard."

Herb sat down opposite David. "I know this may be none of my business but there have been rumors running through the team."

"There are always rumors," he said reviewing the team schedule.

"But this one has to do with you and Stephanie."

David looked up. "What rumor?"

"That you and Stephanie have something going on."

"Of course we do. She's my star at the moment and we work together. Nothing more, nothing less."

"Well according to the rumor mill it's more than that.

Apparently, Stephanie has been talking to some of her teammates."

David clenched his jaw. "There's nothing to it."

Herb looked at him for a moment then stood. "I just thought you should know. It wouldn't be good for you or the team if that got out."

"Yeah, thanks. And don't always believe what you hear." He forced a smile.

"Sure." Herb walked out.

David slammed his palm down on the desk. "Dammit." He reached for the phone and dialed Stephanie's number. It rang and rang until it went to her voice mail. David didn't bother to leave a message.

He frowned looking off into space. He should have known better. He was thinking with the wrong head when it came to Stephanie and it could potentially blow up in his face. He shoved the schedule into the desk drawer, got up, grabbed his jacket and stormed out. He would settle this thing with Stephanie once and for all. He had enough problems as it stood. Kelly'd called him early that morning to let him know she was in town and she wanted all of her contracts. He'd deal with Kelly later. She said she'd be at his office around noon. First things first.

When he arrived at the complex where Stephanie lived he slowed. His heart raced. Police cars with lights flashing had blocked off the area. Slowly he got out of the car and walked up to the yellow tape that boldly announced "Crime Scene" in thick black letters. A small curious crowd had gathered.

David got the attention of one of the officers.

"What happened?"

"Who are you?"

"David Livingston. Has something happened to Stephanie?"

The officer stared at him then turned to one of the detectives. "Vinny!" He waved him over. Vinny approached.

"Yeah?"

"This guy is asking about the victim."

Bile rose to David's throat at the word *victim.*

Vinny looked at David. "Who are you?"

David repeated his name. "I'm her coach."

Vinny lifted the yellow tape. "Come with me."

David followed behind the detective. Just as he approached Stephanie's front door a woman in the crowd who was being questioned shouted and pointed. "That's him! He's the one I was telling you about."

David froze. Vinny turned and saw the look of panic on David's face. Vinny frowned.

"This is the man you saw coming out of the house?" Vinny asked the woman.

"Yes, that's him. I wouldn't forget his face." She glared at David.

Vinny took David by the arm then said to the cop taking the statement, "Get her down to the precinct and get her statement down on paper." Then to David, "You have the right to remain silent. Anything you say can and will be used against you in a court of law..."

Vinny tugged David's hands behind his back and put the handcuffs on him. "You have the right to an attorney. If you cannot afford one, an attorney will be appointed for you. Do you understand these rights?"

Everything after that was a blur.

* * *

Kelly was preparing to leave her house and go to training headquarters when she passed by the television and stopped cold.

The scene before her was surreal. She stepped closer to the set to make sure her eyes weren't playing games with her. That was David being taken away in handcuffs. She quickly scanned the room for the remote and turned up the volume.

"Gold medal hopeful Stephanie Daniels was found dead in her town house this morning by police who received a call from a concerned neighbor. Police have just arrested David Livingston, the coach of the team, as a primary suspect in the death."

Her hand flew to her mouth. "Oh my God." What should she do? Who should she call?

Her phone rang. Alex!

She snatched up the phone. "Hello?"

"Ms. Maxwell what are your feelings about the death of your competitor Stephanie Daniels?" the voice asked.

She slammed down the phone. The reporters were after her already. She went to the window. A news van was camped out on the street in front of her house.

How did they even know she was back? She shook her head in disgust and dropped the curtain back in place. Nothing was safe from news hungry reporters.

She went back in the living room and dialed Alex's cell phone. His voice mail came on. She left him an urgent message to call her as soon as possible.

Kelly paced as she tried to figure out what to do. How could this have happened? David killed Stephanie? She couldn't put it together in her head. It didn't make sense.

Why would he do that? She'd just spoken to him that morning. He'd sounded annoyed but had agreed to meet her.

Well, she certainly was not going to be held captive in her own house. She picked up her purse, checked to make sure she had her cell phone then went out to face the press.

The instant she stepped out her door, three reporters came gunning for her.

"Ms. Maxwell. Did you hear about the murder?

"What are your feelings?"

"Do you think he did it?"

"Were they having an affair?"

"When did you get back in town?"

She ignored all the questions and jumped into her Navigator, hoping that it would start right up after having been idle for so long.

The reporters swarmed the truck, banging on the window as she started the engine and backed out of the driveway.

By the time she cleared the block she was shaking like a leaf, checking her rearview mirror every few seconds to monitor the cars behind her.

Her cell phone rang as she pulled up to the light.

She depressed the button on her headset. "Hello?"

"Hey, babe. What's up?"

"Oh, Alex!" She nearly broke down and cried as she babbled what had occurred.

"Are you all right?" he asked, Kelly being his only concern.

"Just shook up." She sniffed.

The news van was right behind her.

She made the next right toward the training facility. At least there she knew security would keep them out.

"Look, I'm going to rearrange my schedule and get on a flight out there as soon as I can."

The idea of having Alex at her side calmed the jangles in her stomach. "Let me at least find out what's going on first. I'm on my way to the camp now."

"Dammit, I knew you shouldn't have gone back there. There's no way you're not going to get swept up in this mess."

"I'm here now. And I'll deal with it."

Alex blew out a frustrated breath. "You call me the minute you know what's going on. And if you don't have to stay I want you back here."

"I know you don't want to hear this, but I want to be here for David. He may be a lot of things but…I do owe him."

"What! After all he's done to you over the years and you haven't even seen the fine print in your contracts yet." His voice boomed through the phone.

"I'm staying. I hope you'll understand."

"And if I don't?" he challenged.

She didn't want to deal with that possibility at the moment. "I'll call you." She disconnected the call.

When she arrived at the training camp reporters and police surrounded it. She showed her ID at the gate and drove onto the grounds.

She went directly to the main office. The team was gathered just outside David's office. Someone she didn't recognize was talking to them.

"Right now we don't know much," he was saying. "They've taken David into custody."

Murmurs danced around the group.

Marcia noticed Kelly standing in the back of the crowd. "Kelly."

All eyes turned in her direction.

Herb stepped through the group. He stuck out his hand. "I'm Herb Townes, the new assistant coach."

"Kelly Maxwell."

"I didn't know you were coming back today. David said a couple of weeks."

"I know. I had to..." She looked around at the expectant faces. She lowered her voice. "Can I speak with you?"

Herb nodded, put his hand on her shoulder and guided her inside his office. "Excuse me everyone." He waited until the team members stepped back before closing the door.

"What happened?" Kelly asked immediately.

Herb blew out a sigh and ran his hand across his short hair. "All I pretty much know is that they've arrested David, and Stephanie is dead."

Kelly slowly sat down. "I spoke to him this morning and told him I was coming over."

"Stephanie hasn't been to practice in several days. I asked him about that this morning. He told me he gave her a few days off, said she needed the rest."

"I can't believe that David would do something like that. It's all an ugly mistake. It has to be."

"I'm sure once the police do a thorough investigation everything will be cleared up."

Kelly nodded.

There was a knock on the door.

"Yes," Herb barked. "Come in."

The door eased open. Marcia poked her head in. "Sorry, but a Detective Scotto is here. He wants to talk to you."

Herb opened his mouth but didn't say anything. He looked at Kelly. "Uh, send him in."

Kelly got up. "I'll wait outside." She got to the door as soon as Vinny Scotto arrived. She tried to walk around him. He looked her over from head to toe then pointed a finger at her.

"Maxwell, right? Kelly Maxwell."

She nodded and tried to keep going.

"I'm going to need to speak with you, too."

"Me? Why?"

"You're a member of this team right?"

"Yes, but—"

"All the team members are being asked to hang around for questioning. So I guess that means you, too." He shifted the toothpick from one side of his mouth to another.

Kelly swallowed. "Fine."

She walked out and was quickly surrounded by her teammates. She assured them all that she was fine and was planning on returning for training shortly. The conversation quickly shifted to David and that's when she heard about the alleged affair.

The group grew quiet when the office door opened and Detective Scotto stepped out followed by Herb.

Herb raised his hands above his head to get everyone's attention. "Detective Scotto has something he wants to say."

"As of right now every member on this team is being told not to leave the vicinity. My partner will be getting everyone's name and contact information. You'll be called into the station individually for questioning."

Discordant grumbles and cries of disbelief were directed at Vinny Scotto.

"We'll try to make the process as quick as possible. I'm sure that each of you want to help get to the bottom of what happened. There may be information you have that you are unaware of. It's our job to get that information." He glanced around at each of the faces. "I expect everyone's cooperation." He turned to Herb. "We'll be in touch." He walked away.

Kelly felt as if she'd stepped into a nightmare and couldn't wake up.

Everyone was talking at once.

Herb held up his hands over his head. "Listen up folks. The officer is going to take everyone's names and contact information. They'll let you know when you have to come in for questioning."

"What's gonna happen to Coach Livingston?" one of the guys asked.

"The team lawyer is working on that now. When I know something more, I'll let everyone know. In the meantime, just line up at the door to my office." He turned to Kelly. "I'm sorry you had to come back to all this."

"Is it true about him and Stephanie?" she asked in a whisper.

Herb slowly shook his head. "I wish I knew for sure."

A police officer stepped to the front of the group and Herb ushered him inside where he started taking information from each of the team members.

By the time Kelly was finally able to leave the training camp several hours later she was exhausted. She returned home and immediately turned on the news. The broadcast showed pictures of David being taken away in handcuffs earlier that morning and updated it with information stating that a witness had identified him as the man she saw coming out of Stephanie's apartment following a loud argument. The reporter went on to say that there were distinct bruises on her neck and there were signs of sexual activity. An autopsy was scheduled for the following day.

Stephanie Daniels was the reigning hopeful for the gold medal, this following an injury to the team's female track star Kelly Maxwell. However, Maxwell had returned to Atlanta and was seen going to the training camp earlier today. Her return would knock Stephanie Daniels back into the second slot. Police are investigating that angle as well. In the meantime, David Livingston was being held without bail.

Kelly turned off the television, feeling ill. Were they implying that she had some hand in Stephanie's death for her own personal gain? She pressed her hands to her temples. This was insane.

Her phone rang. With great reluctance she picked it up.

"Ms. Maxwell?"

"Yes."

"This is Detective Scotto, we met earlier today."

"Yes."

"I'd like you to come down to the Thirtieth Street stationhouse tomorrow morning around eleven. Does that work for you?"

She swallowed over the knot in her throat. "I'll be there."

"Good, see you then."

Her head began to pound and she did something she hadn't done in weeks, she stuffed herself with sweets and got rid of it all as soon as it went down.

Chapter 39

Dodging the gauntlet of reporters on her way to the station was exhausting enough, but nothing compared to the questioning posed by Detective Scotto.

"Make yourself comfortable Ms. Maxwell," Scotto said, as he sipped on his cup of coffee. "Hopefully this won't take too long."

Kelly took a seat at the long scarred gray metal table and folded her hands in her lap.

"What exactly is your relationship to David Livingston?" he began right away.

"He's my coach."

"Is that it?"

"I don't know what you mean."

"Is that all he is to you—your coach?"

"Yes, of course."

"Hmm. There seems to be some question about that." He looked at her.

"There shouldn't be. There is nothing going on with us if that's what you're trying to imply."

He sat down and flipped open a folder. "I see from my notes that he's been your guardian since you were sixteen years old is that correct?"

Her heart thumped. "Yes."

"So he is more than just your coach."

She didn't respond.

"Would you say that the two of you had a special relationship?"

"I was very grateful to him for helping me, yes."

"Grateful enough to ensure that you didn't disappoint him in any way?"

"I don't know what you're talking about."

"I think you do." He closed the folder and leaned forward, stared her in the eyes. "Having a winning team translates into millions of dollars for the team and for the coach. Isn't that right?"

"Yes, but—"

"And you would get a big portion of that with endorsements and sponsorship. Is that right?"

"Yes. I—"

"In other words you have a lot to gain by reclaiming your spot on the team and an awful lot to lose if you didn't."

Kelly felt warm all over. She laced her fingers together and squeezed them to keep from shaking. "Detective Scotto, if you have all that information then you know that I've been gone from Atlanta for almost two months taking rehab in New York for a broken ankle. I haven't seen Stephanie since before I left."

"But you have seen Coach Livingston. He was living with you at your hotel in New York and only recently returned after the assistant coach suffered a heart attack." He smiled at the surprise in her eyes. "Yes, I do my homework, Ms. Maxwell. I also know that he made a recent trip to see you again and then you return to Atlanta, unannounced, and Stephanie Daniels is found dead. With her out of the way, your spot on the team would be in the bag as they say."

Kelly's eyes widened with alarm. "You aren't accusing me of killing Stephanie?"

"Hmm, we'll leave that for the District Attorney to decide. The M.E. is still running tests to determine the cause of death, but in the meantime, I need to do my part."

"Is your part tossing out false accusations?" she fumed.

"My part is getting to the truth, no matter how ugly it may be. You may not like it, but it's my job."

She wanted to slap the smug look off his face. "If that's the case then I think you need another day job." She pushed back in her chair and stood. "If you don't have any other accusations to make I'll be leaving now."

Vinny stood. "Of course. You're free to go. I'm sure we'll be talking again. And you know you can't leave the jurisdiction."

She threw him a nasty look. "Have a great day, Detective." She snatched up her purse from the table and walked out praying that she wouldn't collapse in a heap on the way.

When she reached her truck her cell phone was beeping. She checked her messages and there was one from Alex. She got in and turned on the ignition but couldn't find the energy to pull off. She sat there for a few moments. She hadn't spoken to Alex since their falling out and just the sound of his voice on the message was enough to ease the tightness in her stomach.

She dialed his number and hoped that he'd pick up. The voice mail answered. She squeezed her eyes shut in disappointment, but left him a long message trying to bring him up to date but mostly to let him know how much she missed him and needed to talk to him.

With that done, she put her phone back in her purse and drove off.

When she reached her house the message light was flashing on her phone. With all that had transpired in the last forty-eight hours there was no telling who might be calling.

She sat down on the couch and pressed the flashing light. Two calls were from reporters who wanted an exclusive interview. One was a telemarketer and the last one sent a chill through her.

It was from Steven Mobley the Atlanta Sports Commission liaison. He wanted everyone from the team to come in for mandatory drug testing. Her test was scheduled for the following morning.

She jumped at the sound of her ringing phone. With shaky hands she picked it up.

"Hello?"

"Baby, it's me."

"Oh, Alex, thank God."

"How are you, what's going on?"

She brought him up to date as best she could, leaving nothing out.

"I can't believe that they think you had something to do with this."

"Neither can I."

"I know this is hard, but it's only a matter of time before they sort this all out."

"I know. It's just the waiting that's so unnerving."

"Listen about the other day, I'm sorry for overreacting. I had no right to go off on you like that. Of course you and David have a lot of history together. You wouldn't be the woman that I've fallen in love with if you'd behaved any other way."

"I'm sorry, too. I know my relationship with David is anything but conventional and I shouldn't have assumed that you would take it without reacting. If you did, a girl might think you didn't care." She laughed lightly.

"Friends?"

"Friends."

Alex paused a moment. "I think I'd better tell you this next bit of news before the press gets wind of it. It's part of the reason why I called."

"Oh no, what else could it be?"

"Charisse is Stephanie's cousin."

"What!"

"She called me this morning. Apparently, Charisse is listed as next of kin and she was notified."

"The world is getting smaller by the minute," she replied drolly.

"There's more."

"I don't know if I want to hear it."

"She's on her way down there. You're liable to run into her at some point. I didn't want you to be taken by surprise."

"Nothing surprises me at this point, Hutch. Can you come down here? I don't want to deal with all this alone."

"I've already made arrangements to be there by Saturday morning. Just hang in there, babe. It's gonna be all right."

"I'll meet you at the airport."

He gave her his flight information.

"I don't know if I can last two more days," she confessed, bone and brain weary.

"You will. Just try to relax and do what they ask."

"I know." She sighed.

"Get some rest. I'll call you later tonight."

"All right. I think I'll lay down for a while."

"Oh, were you able to get your documents?"

"No. I have no idea where David kept them. I feel so stupid."

"Don't. Don't beat yourself up. You trusted him and you had no reason not to trust him. It's as simple as that. We'll get it all straightened out."

"I'm gonna hold you to that," she said, forcing some cheer into her voice.

"You got it. Listen I have to run. I have a conference in about ten minutes."

"Okay. Call me later. Don't forget."

He chuckled. "I'll definitely try not to forget to call you."

She laughed. "Talk to you later."

"Later."

"And Hutch," she said quickly.

"Yes?"

"I love you."

"Love you, too. Bye for now."

"Bye." She hung up the phone.

She rested her head back against the cushions of the couch. Charisse was coming to town: her man's baby's mama and cousin to her now dead rival and teammate. Could life get any stickier than this? If it weren't so twisted she would laugh, but there was nothing even remotely funny.

Chapter 40

Here we are now

Kelly arrived at the clinic shortly before ten a.m., the damning words from the newspaper still spinning around in her head. *Gold Medal Hopeful Stephanie Daniels Found Dead in her Atlanta Apartment... Now it appears with Maxwell on the mend and her competitor no longer a threat, Maxwell may well gain back her title of the golden girl.*

David had been released on bail and called her that morning. He tried to assure her that everything was going to be all right, that he had nothing to do with Stephanie's death and now these stories of steroid use on the team. He begged her to believe him, but she didn't know what to believe anymore.

She went to the front desk. "I'm scheduled for a test," she said to the nurse.

The nurse looked up from the charts in front of her and smiled. "Name?"

"Kelly Maxwell."

The nurse eyed her for a moment then typed some information into the computer. She looked up at Kelly. "Room 610. Down the hall, second door on the left."

"Thanks."

Kelly entered the room. There were two nurses and a guy in a suit. He was the typical looking bureaucrat. Medium build, pale complexion with sandy brown hair, a nondescript face and a suit right off the rack.

"Ms. Maxwell?" the man in the suit said.

Kelly nodded. "Yes."

"Have a seat. I'm Steven Mobley from the Sports Commission. I have some papers here that I need you to sign before you're tested."

"Papers?"

"Yes. Attesting to the fact that if steroids are found in your blood you agree that you will be removed from the team as a violation of the rules set by the Commission." He handed her the papers. "Look them over and sign them. Then we can get started with the tests."

Kelly took the papers, at least mildly thankful that her hands were not shaking. She looked them over and the words began to run around on the page. Nothing made sense. She was in the throes of an episode. All of the tension and stress had finally gotten to her. She drew in a deep breath, forcing herself to remain calm. She closed her eyes for a moment evoking visions of sandy beaches and brilliant blue waves rushing against the shore. She breathed in again, allowing her mind to take inventory of her body, section by section until she was relaxed. She drew in another deep breath.

"Ms. Maxwell," Mr. Mobley barked.

Kelly wouldn't let his tone affect her. She tuned him out and concentrated for a few seconds more on being completely relaxed. Slowly she opened her eyes.

He was scowling at her and the two nurses looked at her curiously.

"Migraine," she said before focusing on the papers in her hands. The words made sense. Inwardly she smiled. She signed where indicated. The last thing she had to worry about was steroids.

Mobley oversaw the drawing of blood and labeling of the tubes and then she was free to go.

The moment she stepped outside cameras and popping flashbulbs were in her face.

"Ms. Maxwell, were you here to be tested for steroid use?"

"Are steroids the reason for your phenomenal performance on the track?"

"Was Coach Livingston administering steroids to the team?"

"What are your feelings about Stephanie Daniels's use of steroids?"

Kelly pushed her way past them trying to hide her face as she hurried across the parking lot to her truck. The questions and the reporters followed her. She was barely able to get inside her truck and it wasn't until she gunned the engine that they finally made room for her to drive off.

What in the world was going on? She knew that in the sports world random drug testing was the norm and with so many athletes taking steroids the commission had really cracked down. But the press had gotten wind of something.

She drove as quickly as the law allowed back to her house and prayed that the reporters felt like preying on someone else, at least long enough for her to get inside her door. No such luck.

She rode past a tight knot of cameramen and print reporters who were camped out in front of her house. She got out, looked each of them in the eye as they fired questions at her. She ignored them all and went inside.

Once on the other side of the door, she leaned back against it and gave in to the fatigue and anxiety. She slid down the door drawing her knees up to her chest. She lowered her head and closed her eyes. She should have listened to Alex. She should have stayed in New York.

Finally she pulled herself up from the floor and went to her bedroom. She stripped out of her clothes then went to run a hot bath.

Almost an hour later she emerged, feeling somewhat better. She fixed herself a light meal and settled down in front of the television.

At the top of the news was the Stephanie Daniels death. The M.E.'s report was back and the toxicology tests indicated that there were high levels of steroids found in the deceased's blood. There was reason to believe that David Livingston, the team coach and prime suspect in Ms. Daniels's death, may have provided the steroids not only to Ms. Daniels but the rest of the team. Several substances were removed from his home after a search warrant was issued.

Kelly aimed the remote at the television and turned it off. This was worse than a nightmare.

* * *

The next time Kelly came out of her house was to go to the airport to pick up Alex. The newshounds had dwindled down to less than a half-dozen as she zoomed past them wishing she could mow them down without having charges brought against her.

As usual airport security was tight. She had to circle the airport twice before she spotted Alex standing near the curbside pickup.

A warm feeling of peace filled her when she saw him. The knot that had been in her stomach for days slowly loosened and she smiled for the first time in what felt like far too long. She pulled up in front of him.

Alex opened the door, tossed his bag in the back seat and hopped in.

"Don't move," he said.

She frowned. "Why, what's wrong?"

"I just want to look at you for a minute."

She giggled.

"You're still as beautiful as I remembered." He leaned close and kissed her with such tenderness that Kelly's chest ached. Slowly he eased back and caressed her cheek. "God I missed you."

"I missed you, too," she whispered.

A security guard tapped on the window. "You can't stay here," he said.

Kelly rolled her eyes, and eased out onto the exit road. "How was the flight?"

"Not bad. Lousy food, of course."

"Well, I'll fix us something when we get back to my place." She glanced at him. "I think I should warn you that you're going to have to run the gauntlet of reporters when we get there. They've been living outside my house since I got back in town."

"Oh boy, that bad huh?"

"Yes, this is big news, at least until something else piques their interest."

"Have you heard anything new?"

"No. Just waiting for the tests results to come back, which should be any day now."

He put his hand on her thigh. "How are you, really?"

"Exhausted, frustrated." She turned to him. "But I'm a helluva lot better now that you're here."

"Well, I took a short leave. So I'm here for as long as you need me."

"You don't know how glad I am to hear that."

When they arrived at her house, the news van was still parked outside and several reporters were milling about. They came to attention when her truck approached.

"Here we go," she said.

He took her hand. "I'm here now." He reached into the back seat and took his bag then got out. He came around to her side and opened her door. When she stepped out he put his arm around her shoulders and walked her to the door, shielding her from the onslaught of flashbulbs and questions.

"Whew!" he breathed once they'd shut the door behind them. "You've been dealing with this all week?" He peeked out of the window.

"Everywhere I go. Don't be surprised if you see your face in the papers tomorrow as some sort of accomplice."

"Unreal."

"Let me show you around so you can relax and get comfortable." She took his hand and walked him through the rooms. "Make yourself at home," she said, when they got to her bedroom.

"I like the sound of that." He gave her a wink.

Kelly giggled. "You can use the top drawer and put whatever you want in the closet. And you can—"

He swept her into his arms and looked down into her upturned face. "When this is all behind us, I thought we could take a trip somewhere."

"Have somewhere in mind?"

"A deserted island. Just me and you."

"Hmm, Dr. Hutchinson that sounds very naughty."

"You haven't seen naughty."

He ran his hands along her back until her body curved into his. His lips found hers and he moaned into the sweetness of her mouth. Then like a scene from *An Officer and a Gentleman,* he swept her up into his arms. She almost expected to hear applause when he carried her across the room and laid her down on the bed. He lay down beside her, kissing her, holding her, telling her how much he missed her, how much he loved her, all the while removing her clothes.

When she was fully naked he began his worship of her body, starting at her head, and worked his way down her body, with a slow intensity that had Kelly's senses reeling. His mouth and hands worked in tandem alternately arousing every inch of her exposed flesh with hot kisses and titillating caresses.

Her fingers fumbled with the buttons of his shirt but finally got them undone. Then she went to work on the belt and zipper. He pulled off his loosened clothing and tossed them on the floor next to Kelly's. She drew in a sharp breath when she felt the power of his erection pressing against her thigh. He was rock hard and just the thought of him inside her again set her own juices flowing.

Alex played with her clit until she trembled, her hips instinctively arching in preparation and when he slid two fingers inside her she climaxed with such a powerful force she saw lights dancing behind her lids. She called his name over and again. Her body shook, her hips rose and fell against the pressure of his fingers wanting more. Without removing his hand he moved above her and spread her thighs wide. He reached for a pillow and pushed it under her hips so that they rose at a high angle. She wasn't sure how but at some point he'd put on a condom. He draped her legs over his shoulders and let his tongue finish what his fingers had started.

And just when she thought she would pass out from pleasure he filled her in one long, stiff thrust. All the air rushed from her lungs and she swore she could feel him in the bottom of her stomach.

Alex rode her slow and deep wanting to hit every spot. He reached between the pillow and her hips and pulled her even closer to him so that he couldn't move in and out of her, only rotate his pelvis until they were both delirious with the pleasure they were getting and giving.

He kissed her hard like a man who was beyond reason, darting his tongue in and out of her mouth taking her breath away. Then he pulled back, lowered his head to her breasts and caught her hard nipple between his teeth and sucked and sucked.

"Oh…my…God…" She lifted her legs higher until they were around his neck and he was in her as deep as he could go. Heat raced through her and the electric currents running from her breasts to her legs was more than she could take.

It didn't seem possible but he pushed further, hit that spot that she'd only read about and she lost her mind. The powerful explosion that ripped through her shot back at Alex and he went entirely stiff as he came from the soles of his feet until every drop was gone.

By the time they'd pulled themselves together enough to do more than murmur and snuggle, the sun had already set. They were in a tangle of limbs and damp sheets.

"I feel utterly decadent," Kelly said.

"I love decadent. Don't you," Alex murmured and nuzzled her neck. His stomach grumbled.

Kelly giggled. "You need to be fed."

"I have something I'd love to taste again."

"Alex Hutchinson if you touch me in less than two hours from now I'm going to have to hurt you," she warned. She tried to scramble from the bed, but he grabbed her around the waist before she could escape.

"Don't deny a starving man," he pleaded, nibbling her back and Kelly erupted into a fit of laughter as he tickled her ribs.

"No fair," she squealed.

"My sentiments exactly." He flipped her over as if she weighed no more than a newborn. He looked down at her, pecked her lightly on the lips. "I'll give you a play this time." He rolled off her. "But it's only because you wore me out, girl."

"I wore you out!"

"Exactly. Look at me. I'm half the man I was."

Kelly rolled her eyes upward. "In your dreams." She got out of bed and half walked, half dragged herself into the bathroom. She used the toilet and stood for a moment looking at her reflection in the mirror. She was actually glowing as if an inner light had been set.

She ran hot water in the sink and gave herself a quick bird bath, enough to feel comfortable while she fixed them something to eat. She turned toward the door and Alex was standing there watching her as she was putting on the robe that she kept in the bathroom.

"Humph, humph, humph. Girl, the things I could do with you in that shower."

She wagged a finger at him. "Don't even think about it."

"Okay you win. Two hours."

Kelly chuckled. "Come on, let me see how good you are in the kitchen."

They sat opposite each other after preparing grilled salmon, yellow rice and Caesar salad.

A single white taper sat on the center of the table. Luther Vandross's *Live at Radio City Music Hall* CD played in the background.

"I was at that concert," Alex said. "It was his last one before his stroke."

"What a loss," Kelly murmured. She angled her head to the side. "Wasn't that his Valentine's Day concert?"

"Hum, uh."

"Who'd you go with?"

He looked up, the fork midway between the plate and his mouth. He put the fork down on the plate. "Charisse."

Kelly lifted her chin. "Oh." She focused on her food. "Have you thought any more about...your situation with Charisse?"

He pushed his plate aside, his appetite gone. "She's going to keep the baby. That's what she told me before I left New York. So...I'm going to be a father." He pushed up from the table and rubbed his hand across the stubble that was forming on his chin. "How do you feel about that?" It took a moment for the shock to become manageable before she could form a coherent thought.

"I wish things were different. I wish it hadn't happened. I wish it was me and not some other woman. But none of those things are true. When I said I wanted to build this relationship it was with the full knowledge of what I was walking into." She stood up and walked over to him. She put her hands around his waist. "You stood by me, you helped to turn my life around. You could have kept going when you found out about my dyslexia and the eating disorder, not to mention all the mess with David. And now," she laughed without humor, "I'm being looked at as a suspect in a death. Can't get much more serious than that." She took a breath. "I love you, Hutch. What happened between you and Charisse didn't happen on my watch. I know you will do what is needed for Charisse and your child, and I'll be there by your side as long as you want me there."

Alex gathered her close, and kissed the top of her head. "That's why I love you," he said softly.

"One day at a time," she said reaching up to kiss his lips. "One day at a time." She kissed him again. "Let's finish dinner. There's something that I want to talk to you about. Something that I've been working on."

Chapter 41

David sat in his living room with his attorney, Melvin Walker.

"It doesn't look good, David. I have to be honest with you. At worst, they can indict you for murder. At the least they have you on the steroid rap." He took off his glasses and rubbed the bridge of his nose. "I have to ask you this." He paused. "Did you kill Stephanie Daniels?"

"No. I swear I didn't." He got up from the dining room chair and began to pace. "We had…a thing. I know it was stupid. But I didn't kill her."

"So what about the loud argument the neighbor heard?"

David blew out a breath. "We had a fight. She was… crazed. I can't explain it. I'd never seen her like that before. I…grabbed her, tried to keep her off me. But I swear, when I left she was as much alive as me and you."

Mel nodded. "And what about the steroids they found in your apartment?"

David lowered his head in shame. "I got them from a supplier in Smyrna."

"Did you give them to Stephanie?"

"No! Absolutely not. I…gave them to Kelly Maxwell," he confessed.

Kelly slowly hung up the phone. She and Alex had built their own private island within the confines of her apartment over the past two days. But that idyll had just been shattered.

"You want to tell me what has you looking so panicked?" Alex asked walking over to her. He took the phone from her hand and hung it up.

"That was Mr. Mobley from the Sports Commission," she said as if in a trance.

"And?"

She sat down then looked up into Alex's concerned face. "He said my tox screen came back positive for steroids and that I'll be brought up on charges." She covered her mouth with her hand.

"There has to be a mistake."

"I…I can't believe it. I've never taken anything."

Alex rushed off to the bathroom and pulled her medication bottles off the shelf. One by one he opened them. He frowned when he looked at the bottle filled with what should have been her calcium supplements. He brought the bottle back to her and showed her the contents.

"These are not your pills."

She snatched them from his hand. "What are you talking about? These are what I picked up from the pharmacy from the prescription that you wrote."

"Trust me, these are not what I prescribed."

"Then…"

"Who filled the prescription?"

She thought back to the day in the pharmacy and how adamant she was about taking care of it herself and the argument with David that followed. "I did," she murmured.

"Well, one of two things happened, either we have an idiot behind the counter that is pushing illegal drugs or your pills were changed."

"David?"

"He had access."

"But why?"

"Steroids have incredible powers. They increase muscle mass, physical strength, build adrenaline, the list goes on, not to mention the downside. They alter personality as well, making the user overly aggressive. Over time they can cause heart and kidney damage."

"David—" she shook her head "—he wouldn't do that to me. For what reason?"

"He wanted you back on that track. He wanted a winner." Alex hung his head. "I should have known. Your recovery from that kind of injury was remarkable to say the least."

"So you're saying without these drugs I wouldn't have gotten better?"

"I'm going to be honest with you." He looked her in the eye. "In my professional opinion, you would have never run again, not competitively. I simply thought I was wrong. I wanted to be wrong so I didn't…" He slammed his fist into his palm. "I didn't think of doing a toxicology screening." He sat back. "I want to tell you something, something I should have shared with you a long time ago…."

Slowly he told her about Leigh Wells, and his subsequent bout with alcohol. "I blamed myself. I thought I should have been able to make her well, go against everything that I knew to be true about her injury. And when I finally told her the truth...she couldn't deal with it, couldn't deal with the reality that she would be crippled for the rest of her life. She blamed me for giving her false hopes, filling her head with promises that I ultimately was unable to keep. I didn't want that to ever happen again. Not with you, Kelly, not with us."

"You never lied to me." She took his face in her hands. "You never gave me false hope." She paused then added, "I'm not Leigh, baby."

His gaze ran over her face. He saw past all the flaws and the mismatched features to the genuine spirit beneath, to the woman who had captured his heart and soul. To him she was the most beautiful woman in the world. "I love you, Kelly."

"I know and I love you, too."

"We'll get through this. All of this."

"One day at a time."

He took her hands. "We need to go to the police with this information about your pills."

She lowered her head. "I know. I don't want to turn on David...yes, even after all of this. I want him to have the chance to come clean." She looked into his eyes. "Can you understand that?"

"I don't like it but I understand. So what do you want to do?"

"I want to meet with him, face-to-face."

"It will be a media circus."

"I know." She bit down on her bottom lip in thought.

"Maybe this time we can let the media work for us instead of against us."

"How?"

"I have an idea."

Chapter 42

"Are you ready?" Alex asked as they sat hand in hand in David's attorney's office.

"Who can ever be ready for something like this? I'm as ready as I can be."

He squeezed her hand and leaned over and kissed her lips. "Did I tell you how proud I am of you?"

She smiled. "No. Tell me."

"Kelly Maxwell I am incredibly proud of you, more than you will ever know. What you're about to do takes heart, determination and plenty of guts. All of which you have enough of to share with the world."

Her eyes filled with tears. She sniffed. "You're gonna make a girl ruin her makeup in front of millions."

"You'd still be beautiful." He wiped a tear from beneath her eyes.

Mel opened the door to his office and stuck his head in. "We're ready."

Kelly drew in a deep breath. "Where's David?"

"He's already out front."

Kelly nodded and stood. Together she and Alex went out to face the media.

When they entered the atrium of the office building, the entire floor was filled with news crews with their cameras and microphones and curious onlookers. She saw David with his head bowed seated behind the podium that was set up for their announcement.

She and Alex walked up to the seating area. David looked up at her and it appeared that he'd aged ten years since she'd last seen him. In that moment she recalled their first meeting, his persistence, his unwavering belief in her. She remembered him pulling all kinds of strings to get her into a good school, taking care of her, being her friend and mentor. She didn't want to believe that it had all been an illusion rather that there was some truth to the years that they'd spent together. She had to believe that. She sat down and Alex sat next to her, holding her hand tightly.

Mel stepped up to the microphone.

"I want to thank all of you for being here. The past few weeks have been difficult for my client and for everyone involved in this unfortunate incident. As you all know, the medical examiner, yesterday morning, has clearly determined that Stephanie Daniels's death was caused by the ingestion of steroids over a long period of time and the combination of large quantities of alcohol caused the heart attack that killed her. There have been allegations that my client provided the drugs that killed her. That too has been proven to be false." He took a breath and glanced down at his notes. "In the midst of this tragedy, Kelly Maxwell, one of the stars of the track team, has been found to have been using steroids as well, and was subsequently discharged from the team. At this time, I want to let my client David Livingston speak to that." He turned to David and nodded in encouragement.

David approached the podium. He looked over his shoulder at Kelly.

"Thank you," he murmured into the microphone. He lifted his head and looked out onto the faces in the crowd. "For as long as I can remember I wanted to be a coach. I wanted to mold a team that was unbeatable. That ideal became all I lived for at any cost." He looked down then back at the audience. "I allowed my desires to outweigh good sense and it cost me a good friend, my reputation and the career that I love." His voice broke. "As you know, several months ago, Kelly Maxwell sustained a major injury that required surgery and rehabilitation. She was my star, my ticket to my dreams coming true and I didn't want to lose that. I knew the power of steroids...and I switched Ms. Maxwell's supplements with steroid tablets. She knew absolutely nothing about it and should in no way be punished for my selfishness and greed. I will deal with whatever the law sees fit, but I can't let what I did ruin an innocent person." He looked out on the audience one last time. "Thank you." He returned to his seat as flash-bulbs popped and cameras whirred.

Mel turned to Kelly. "Ready?"

She nodded her head and stepped up to the micro-phone. She cleared her throat and took a moment to gather her thoughts.

"I know what David did was wrong and it was illegal,

but he would have never been able to do that...if I had been able to read."

To a stunned audience she told them of her battle with dyslexia and her eating disorder, the struggles that she'd endured over the years, the shame, and the alienation. "Had it not been for my injury and going to New York, and meeting Dr. Alex Hutchinson, I may have never faced or attempted to deal with either of these weights that I've been carrying. I would have simply gone on living a half-life of shame and deceit. I cannot thank him enough for his encouragement and for forcing me to come out from behind the protection of my own illusions. But the only person I was fooling was myself. I've taken charge of my life and I know that what I am dealing with and what thousands of others are dealing with will not fix itself overnight." She looked over her shoulder at Alex who was smiling with pride and encouragement. "It will only happen one day at a time." She drew in a long breath. "I've begun the steps necessary to set up a foundation for athletes and young adults across the country who are dealing with these problems and I will be turning in my track shoes to personally run the foundation. I welcome your prayers, your support and of course donations." She smiled and walked away from the microphone and into Alex's arms.

In the back of the crowd, Charisse listened and watched. What struck her most was not so much what Kelly said, but the look that passed between her and Alex. He'd never looked at her like that and he never would. That much she had finally accepted. She turned to leave before they spotted her. There was nothing for her here. She was going home to pick up her life. She'd done what she'd come there to do. Upon her arrival in Atlanta she'd gone to the police and told them about Stephanie's erratic behavior, which helped to cinch their case about steroid abuse. No, there was nothing for her here.

Epilogue

Six months later, New York City

Kelly had secured her contracts from David and thankfully he hadn't done anything with her money. She could live comfortably for a very long time from the investments that he'd made on her behalf and the residuals from the commercials she'd done. For that she would always be grateful. David would spend some time in jail and pay his fines. Hopefully, he would make it through and come out a wiser man. She'd even offered him a job as a counselor when he got out in a year. In the meantime she still had to work hard on her own issues. It was a lifelong struggle but the value of the counseling and the classes was immeasurable.

She hummed softly as she unpacked boxes in her new

office on Broadway and Fifty-Seventh Street. It was small but would serve her purposes. She'd already hired an assistant, a young woman in graduate school who had plans to go into sports management. She and Alex were pretty much inseparable and she was really liking the whole living together thing. Life was good.

"Hey sweetheart."

Kelly looked up surprised to see Alex in the middle of the day. She wiped her hands on her jeans and walked over to him. "Hey, this is a treat but what are you doing here?" She sat down on the edge of her brand-new desk.

"I got a letter in the mail today…from Charisse."

Kelly's stomach knotted. "What…did it say?"

He drew in a breath. "She is relinquishing all parental rights."

Kelly frowned. "What, why?"

"She wants you and I to raise the baby. She sent the documents in the mail for me to sign. She's due to deliver the baby any day now."

Kelly didn't know what to think or how to feel. She knew that Alex had every intention of being a major part of the child's life but she never expected Charisse to turn the baby over to him totally. "Did she say why?"

"She said that she went through with the pregnancy because termination was not something that she could live with. Her plan, unknown to me, was to have the baby adopted." He reached for her hand. "She was at the press conference. She said when she saw us together she knew that was the kind of loving household she'd want the baby to be raised in."

Kelly blinked several times. She was speechless.

"I wanted to wait until your birthday next month, but…"

He reached into his jacket pocket and took out a velvet box. He opened it and a brilliant marquis diamond sparkled, set on a platinum band. "But if I was going to ask you to be a partner with me, to be mother to my child, I couldn't do that without you saying yes to being my wife first. Will you say yes, Kelly? Will you marry me? I will be good to you girl. I'll love and honor you, trust you with my secrets and guard yours with my life. I'll be your friend, your lover, your partner. Through thick and thin."

Tears slid down her cheeks as she thought of where she'd been, how far she'd come and where she planned to go. She knew it wouldn't be easy, but nothing in her life had ever been except for running. But she wasn't running anymore. She was standing still and tall ready to face life and whatever it dished out and she couldn't dream of anyone other than Alex "Hutch" Hutchinson that she wanted at her side.

She stretched out her left hand and with shaky hands Alex slid the ring on her slender finger. He held her hand.

"I'll love you for the rest of my life," she whispered. "One day at a time."

Dear Reader,

Thanks so much for taking a chance on me again! I do hope that you enjoyed Kelly, Alex and David's story.

When I was asked to do this project, I thought, great—a track star—since I was a runner myself (in my youth!). Of course, to complicate matters, I wanted more than a simple love story about an athlete. Instead, I wanted a story of courage over adversity—not only on the track, but in life. I think you would agree that Kelly had much to deal with. Dyslexia and eating disorders are so very common. Often young children are misdiagnosed and put on behavioral medication instead of being treated for dyslexia. In women, particularly, there is a surge in eating disorders propelled by the false images of what is beautiful. In both instances, stress and the desire to please only make the problems worse.

I hope that I have at least shed some light on these two problems, and hopefully someone out there will realize that there is help and hope and, of course, love!

Until next time,

Donna